I0578706

FRAGILE SAINTS

Fragile Saints

A novel

by

CLAIRE IBARRA

Adelaide Books
New York / Lisbon
2021

FRAGILE SAINTS
A novel
By Claire Ibarra

Copyright © by Claire Ibarra

Cover design © 2021 Adelaide Books

Published by Adelaide Books, New York / Lisbon
adelaidebooks.org

Editor-in-Chief
Stevan V. Nikolic

All rights reserved. No part of this book may be reproduced in any
manner whatsoever without written permission from the author except in
the case of brief quotations embodied in critical articles and reviews.

For any information, please address Adelaide Books
at info@adelaidebooks.org
or write to:
Adelaide Books
244 Fifth Ave. Suite D27
New York, NY, 10001

ISBN: 978-1-954351-74-5
Printed in the United States of America

This is a work of fiction. Names, characters, businesses, places, events,
locales, and incidents are either the products of the author's imagination
or used in a fictitious manner. Any resemblance to actual persons, living
or dead, or actual events is purely coincidental.

For my daughters Celia Rose and Carmen Florencia~

May you always find life's magic.

Acknowledgments

This novel would not have been possible without the support of the creative writing faculty at Florida International University. I especially thank my thesis adviser, Debra Dean, and the director of the creative writing program, Les Standiford, for their insight and guidance.

I would also like to thank my circle of writers and friends who read and offered comments to this work during its formative stages, and Kathie Klarreich for mentoring me along this journey. Much love and appreciation goes to my family for their unwavering encouragement. I am truly grateful to my Peruvian extended family for inspiring this work of fiction.

Excerpts from *Fragile Saints* have been previously published in *Embark Literary Journal* in 2018 and *Still Point Arts Quarterly* in 2020.

Chapter 1

Elsa flipped through the essays piled on her small desk. She had to grade finals, but her mind was still reeling from the student conference she had just had. The student was angry about failing, but he hadn't attended class for the past three weeks. He had pounded his fist on her desk before storming out.

The fluorescent lights in the office gave her a headache. The artificial light seemed to have its own wiry energy field, and it drained her. She peered out the window of the office and could see that it was still raining. There was a blanket of green stretching out beyond the campus and then a wall of redwoods, which stood like an ancient fortress in the distance. She longed to be inside the forest, where the smell of rain and the green could nourish her.

"Hey, there. Heard you had a rough conference." Gary stuck his head inside and looked over Elsa. He added, "Our meeting probably didn't help things. I just wanted to make sure you were okay." Elsa could see the look of pity in his eyes, and this infuriated her. She didn't need his sympathy.

At the meeting, the faculty had been enlightened to the fact that enrollment at their small community college was way down and that major cut backs were in the works. Elsa was informed that she wouldn't have any classes over the summer.

"I'm fine. I'm heading home now." Elsa rose and put the stack of essays into a manila folder. She grabbed her purse.

"Come on, Elsa. I know you better than that. Why are you being so cold?" Gary stood in the doorway, blocking her exit. His black hair was slicked back, and his green eyes glistened like a cat's on the prowl.

"Listen, Gary. I know you're expressing concern, but I'm really tired. It's been a long day." Elsa squeezed by him and strode away. She stopped, turned briefly, and said, "Gary, your good intentions often come too late. But thanks for trying."

Her ex-husband Charles and Gary were best of friends.

Their marriage had ended when Charles had an affair with a student. He wasn't even reprimanded by the school. Elsa had stubbornly stayed at the college, thinking, why should she be the one to leave if she did nothing wrong? Charles should have been fired. Hadn't he broken some kind of ethical code?

Elsa made her way down the hallway and headed toward the elevator. Her heart started pounding. She always felt sure she would bump into Charles. His office was just around the corner.

Soon she was walking down the dank stairwell. This was the best way to avoid an awkward encounter. They had been divorced for a year, and she had become accustomed to slinking down hallways and rushing through the parking lot.

Elsa got into her car and took a deep breath.

She made her way along the winding road. It was dusk, and the rain made the drive slow. Once she pulled onto the dirt road and approached her cabin, she could see the porch light glowing dimly. She had survived another day, and the cabin was her refuge—even if she often felt lonely there. She walked up the wet wooden steps and entered the warmth of her home.

Elsa was pouring herself a glass of wine, when the telephone rang. It was her mother, Josephine.

"Honey, I wanted to let you know that your grandma has taken a turn for the worse," her mother explained in a soft voice. Angelica, Elsa's grandmother in Peru, had been declining in health over the past few months.

Josephine continued, "She is in hospice now, and she has requested to see you. How would feel about going to Peru with your dad?"

Elsa felt moved that her grandmother wanted to see her. It had been several years since she last saw Angelica. She reminded herself that she now had the summer off from teaching. Maybe it would be a chance to break out of her rut since Charles left. Elsa agreed to accompany her father Miguel to Peru.

That night, the rain beat down on Elsa's cabin in the red-woods while ancestors visited her in strange dreams. Real memories of visiting Peru as a child and those haunting dreams were hardly distinguishable. She recalled her grandmother Angelica's large, old house in Lima, and also the country house in the Andes where her great-grandmother lived.

Elsa remembered following her great-grandmother Lucía into the adobe sheds in the backyard of the country house. Beds of silkworms in various stages of their life cycle filled the dank rooms. Moths, dull and gray, laid tiny specks of eggs, smaller than grains of rice. Those specks would hatch into pure white worms that rapidly grew monstrous as they gorged themselves on fresh, green mulberry leaves.

After their ravenous feasting of leaves, and at some instinctual moment, the worms would rise and begin their search for a suitable twig. Elsa's great-uncle José spread out thin branches on the plank beds, and out of their own body's machinery, the worms constructed cocoons resembling perfect, alabaster eggs.

Indian women sat by the fire in the courtyard, while the cocoons were carefully boiled in cauldrons of water, and one cocoon could produce a single silk thread stretching miles, leaving only a dried pupa behind to be used as animal feed.

Six-year-old Elsa would toss the dried out insect larvae to the chickens in the pen. Some cocoons had to be separated out, allowing moths to emerge and mate and then lay fertile eggs before they quickly died, keeping the cycle going indefinitely.

Elsa watched her great-grandmother Lucía, bent and crooked as she spun the wooden spool, winding thin, wispy raw silk into thread. Lucía would ask Elsa to help her untangle the bundles of thread, so Elsa sat on the floor beside her as the old woman rocked back and forth rhythmically in a creaking chair.

And one night, Lucía magically spun her dead husband, Salvatore, out of the silk piles resting at her feet. As she rocked in the old chair, the wooden spool cast him out, and she worked with tired, stiff hands to reel him back in. Salvatore had become a determined, stubborn man.

But his gentler, softer form billowed above her left shoulder, and he cried, "Lucía, Lucía, how could you be so indifferent to that cancer eating away at my stomach, my liver, at all of my pitiful guts?" His figure of silky, translucent threads swayed and stretched.

Elsa watched in amazement and fear, crouched by her great-grandmother's side.

"It was the guilt that made you sick," Lucía replied. "It was guilt that ate away at your insides. My conscience is clear." And to that, his tenuous form quivered, and the threads collapsed into a heap on the floor.

Elsa then helped Lucía gather up the silk bundles from the cold tiles. Lucía tossed them into her basket and slowly made her way through the courtyard strewn with passion fruit vines, past the laundry hung to dry on chords, past the chicken coop and dog's shed. And Elsa watched as Pastor, the three-legged dog, came out of the shadows and followed the shuffle and thump of Lucía's cane up the staircase to her tiny room with its single bed. Lucía's daughter, Angelica, appeared then. Elsa's grandmother was plump and soft, and she had sparkling dark blue eyes. She took Elsa's hand and led her to bed, tucking her in with a kiss to the forehead. Even after Angelica's warm touch, the ghost of her great-grandfather and those strange, pale worms haunted little Elsa's dreams.

One week later, Elsa and Miguel landed in Lima. They took a taxi from the airport. Lima at dawn looked grim and dirty; the desert-like terrain left everything covered in beige dust. They passed the section of beach used as a dump, and Elsa shuddered as she saw children trek across the smoking mounds and the dark green waters foam yellowish white. Elsa watched out the window of the taxi at the auburn visages of people walking down bustling streets and literally dangling out of crowded, dilapidated buses.

She noticed the dry desert cliffs running above the seashore, which they had navigated to get down to the beach when she was a child. She then remembered the smell of the mounds of burning garbage on the street corners, which her *abuela* had cursed at when the city's trash collectors went on strike.

"*Ay, Dios mio*, we are a poor country; they call us third world." Angelica had cursed them when they passed the stinky, black smoking mounds on the sidewalks. "It's the politicians! *Sinverguenzas!* Swines!"

Elsa recalled the constant assortment of noises, bells and horns that had passed by the street in front of the house at every hour of the day. One particular whistle woke them up at

6:30 in the morning, the baker pushing a cart with fresh rolls, and with that began Angelica's busy day. The only bell Elsa had recognized was the ice cream cart, which passed by every after-noon during those summery December weeks of her childhood.

Now they entered the more picturesque Barranco, with its small plazas and colorful houses. The narrow streets were lined with trees and ornate iron gates. They pulled up to the front of the house. It was six in the morning, but already disheveled men pushed carts loaded with newspapers, milk bottles, and sacks of freshly baked bread down the street. The winter morning was gray and damp.

Barranco was a bohemian neighborhood where the country's most cherished artists– musicians, writers, and painters–congregated to live and work. The beloved songwriter and singer Chabuca Granda called it home, and many of her lyrics described the edifices of the neighborhood, like the Bridge of Sighs where lovers met. Mario Vargas Llosa, the famous writer, lived just blocks away from Angelica before he bitterly expatriated and moved to Spain after a failed campaign for the presidency.

Her father rang the buzzer, and Elsa could hear a dog bark and Aunt Lina yell, "*Quieto!*" Lina opened the door, and she hugged them both while nudging them quickly into the house. Elsa hadn't seen her aunt in several years, since the last time she had visited Peru with Charles. In their seven years of marriage, they made only one trip to Peru. They traveled around the country for three weeks, and stayed in the old house in Barranco with Lina and Angelica for several days. Charles had struggled with the language barrier and culture shock. He preferred trips to Napa Valley more than the adventure of South America.

The taxi driver helped carry in the luggage. Lina tipped the man before shooing him out the door. Elsa noticed that her aunt looked tired and haggard, she had aged in just a few years.

"She's been asking for you, Miguel," Lina explained to her brother as she embraced him and tears ran down her swollen, blotched face. She took her brother's hand and led him and Elsa down the hallway to their mother's bedroom.

Angelica was bed-ridden, drifting in and out of consciousness, and was ninety-six after all. She refused to leave her big, colonial house, with its countless bedrooms where her children had grown up.

Elsa stood in the doorway, looking into the dim room and at her grandmother's frail frame reclined in the sagging bed. Angelica was hooked to an IV, and as Elsa scanned the small room, she noticed the bedpan and a musty, acrid smell. A large crucifix hung over the headboard, and a framed portrait of the Bleeding Heart of Christ presided in one corner of the room. Elsa felt the weight of her grandmother's impending passing, of Angelica's suffering.

Elsa thought back to her childhood visits to her grandmother's big, boisterous house. Elsa had always carried the basket as she walked with Angelica to the market in the mornings. Her *abuela* rattled on in a singsong *castellano* that Elsa could barely decipher. And then there were the meals that Angelica had prepared with one course after another. Elsa and her baby brother would sit at the big, long family table, their feet dangling, as she served them warm, nurturing foods like cream of squash soup, chicken soufflé, and rice pudding doused in cinnamon.

When visiting their grandmother's house, they had been invited into another era, another world where time passed slowly, where family was abundant, and Angelica's doting, maternal instincts oozed out of her like honey from a hive.

"Children, eat," she encouraged them while serving generous second helpings. "I want to see my grandchildren *muy gorditos.*" Their bellies stuck out of their shirts and she smiled. Being chubby in Peru was a compliment, and parents called their children *gorditos* even if they were as skinny as poles.

As Elsa stood in the doorway of Angelica's room, she decided to give her father time alone with his mother. She didn't want to overwhelm Angelica, so Elsa roamed the large house. There were crumbling adobe walls, and the open courtyard was filled with plants beginning to wither and die in solidarity with their housemother. Elsa strolled down the long corridor and peeked into rooms. She peered at the photos in the living room, placed in mismatched frames. There was a photo, nearly faded, of Lucía and Salvatore seated side by side, stately and proud. They both wore serious expressions, and they had made a handsome couple. Elsa looked closer noticing a dark, long shadow looming behind Lucía. It gave Elsa an eerie feeling.

There was another photo that stood out from the others because it was the only one of Angelica and her husband with all their children, three lanky boys and one little girl, Aunt Lina. The family stood squished together, dressed for a beach outing. She took one last glance at the photos of her father as a child. His large brown eyes and pudgy cheeks, and the innocence of childhood apparent on his sweet face, tore at Elsa's heart.

Finally feeling the exhaustion of the trip, Elsa sat down in the dining room.

Aunt Lina walked in just then looking frazzled, tucking loose strands of gray hair back into her bun. Caring for her dying mother was taking a toll on her.

"My dear Elsa. We left you stranded. Angelica woke up long enough to chat with Miguel. I think it's revived her some. Would you like a cup of tea?"

"Don't worry, *Tia*. I can get it myself. I remember that the kitchen's in the back. I'll make us a pot."

"That would be lovely, Elsita. But you must be tired after the flight."

"I don't mind stretching my legs after sitting for so long. It will just take a minute."

Elsa rose and headed down the hall toward the back of the house. There she found the kitchen with its rusty appliances, crooked shelves, and the same old transistor radio on the counter. She filled the tea kettle with water and placed it on the stove. The last time she was in this house, she was with Charles. How strange it felt to be single now. Even though he complained a lot while they were there, she missed his energy, his quirky sense of humor woven through the snarky comments.

Elsa remembered standing in the kitchen with him, as he opened the freezer looking for ice to add to his glass of soda. Charles said, "No luck, I guess the gypsies haven't shown up with the latest modern invention to impress the natives." His sarcasm could be both irritating and amusing at the same time. Elsa let the weight of her loss settle once again and shrugged off the feeling of nostalgia. But the house and Angelica made it hard to shake melancholy.

Later that evening Elsa sat at Angelica's bedside.

Angelica reclined with her head resting on pillows, though she appeared alert and clearheaded. "Is that you, my little Elsa? You are a beautiful, grown woman now." She spoke to Elsa in that same singsong Spanish. "You still have those lovely curls, but your hair isn't pale-yellow anymore." Elsa's hair hadn't been light blonde since she was a girl. Angelica didn't seem to remember Elsa's last visit with Charles.

Elsa stroked her grandmother's fine, white hair and then kissed her forehead. "I missed you, *Abuela*. I was curious about this photograph. It's so lovely and all your children are here."

Elsa handed the framed picture of the family outing to the beach to Angelica, and with a bony finger Angelica stroked each face. "There's an entire lifetime housed in this photograph. My children and so much loss."

"I don't want to make you sad. I hoped the photo would make you happy," Elsa explained.

Angelica whispered, flushed and out-of-breath, as if making her last confession. "Did you know that my father, Salvatore, had another family, with a wife and children, living on the other side of the city? They had no idea he was married to my mother until his funeral, when both our families showed up: two women dressed in mourning and both claiming to be his wife. Imagine their surprise!" She chuckled, the years seeming to have softened the blows of the fiasco.

Elsa was stunned by this revelation; she had no idea. Her father had never talked about it. The story brought to mind those faint recollections of her great-grandmother's spinning of thread, spinning her husband out from fine silk strands–or had it all been a dream? Elsa wasn't sure. Then Elsa recalled Salvatore's desperate pleas to Lucía, his ghostly form woven out of silk threads, at the patio of the country house. His guilt made sense to her now.

Angelica's eyes looked beyond Elsa, as if she were talking to a ghost. Suddenly, she scooted herself upright with the pillows on her bed, and became more animated. Angelica told Elsa that she hadn't been with a man since her husband died. "He was my first and only lover. Is that very unusual?" she asked eagerly.

"It's rare to find that now, *Abuela*. People get married when they're much older these days, if they do at all." Elsa felt tempted to add that most marriages end in divorce. What was the point of her marriage with Charles, especially since they never had children? Elsa wasn't sure if those seven years, even the good ones, were worth the heartache. She wished she could just wipe the slate clean, and recapture time. When she miscarried the first time, she blamed herself. The second time, she was so hurt and angry she blamed Charles. Still, she never imagined that he would betray her, and with one of his students no less. She thought they were grieving together, she thought they would come out the other end stronger, more determined to make it work and have a family. She had even made an appointment at a fertility clinic. Instead, Charles ran away the same year that Elsa turned forty years old.

"Yes, I know that times have changed." Angelica then seemed to drift off, until she said, "I was only thirty-two when Pablo Miguel died of a heart attack. He was young too, it was a genetic condition, you know. Anyway, I think I almost went crazy for a time. I used to dream about him touching me, his hands on my body, and I sometimes woke up crying."

Elsa was taken aback by her grandmother's candor, which made her wonder if Angelica deliberately chose Elsa as a confidant, or if Elsa just happened to be there as these things slipped out, the ramblings of an old, senile woman.

Elsa hadn't been with a man for over a year, since her divorce. She too felt a yearning and desire so great that it filled her with pain, as well as tears. She never expected to share this connection with Angelica.

Elsa would find herself wrestling with an unseen presence, the sheets tangled and damp with her sweat, damp with her desires, only to wake up with tears and sobs. Those were nights she feared being alone for the rest of her life. Those were the nights that she cursed Charles and his younger lover.

Elsa's confidence had been shattered after Charles's affair. She had gone to the college on her day off to pick up some papers, and that's when she saw them leaning against his car.

Charles appeared to have the girl pinned as he kissed her, but the girl didn't resist. Elsa stopped in her tracks, sheepishly went back to her car and drove away. Now she shook off the memory, as Angelica stroked her arm softly.

"You don't have children?" Angelica whispered.

There was the dreaded question. Elsa had prepared herself for this. The Latin culture still valued motherhood and family above all else, even in this day and age. But still, her gut tightened. She whispered back to Angelica, "No, *Abuela.* I don't."

Elsa's thoughts became a mantra. I lost them, it wasn't meant to be, it's better this way.

Angelica was getting tired. She could barely keep her eyes open as she continued, "Maybe I should have remarried, but with all those kids? I guess I didn't really have the time. But listen, *mi niña*, don't be afraid of love. *El Amor*—it comes in all kinds of packages."

The next morning, Elsa sat in a wicker chair in the open corridor reading a book when the nurse emerged from Angelica's room. The nurse, wearing pink uniform scrubs, came twice a day to tend to Angelica.

Elsa called out to her, "How is my grandmother feeling today?"

"She's still dehydrated. Family visits usually perk up patients, lift their spirits, but it's often followed by a bout of exhaustion. She'll probably sleep most of the day."

Elsa waited until the afternoon to enter the dim room and sit once again at Angelica's bedside. Elsa watched her grandmother sleep, listening to her gentle wheezing, noticing the dark purple bruise-like blotches over her translucent, withered skin.

Miguel peeked his head in and asked Elsa, "Lina and I are going downtown for a walk. Would you like to come?"

"I think I'll stay."

"Okay, we'll be back before it gets late."

After a long while of sitting in stillness, Elsa reading her book and Angelica lost in dreams, Angelica began to stir–her arms gently searching at her sides, muttering. "It wasn't his fault, I made him follow me. I sent the letters, but we were only children."

Elsa leaned in and stroked her grandmother's head. "It's all right, *Abuela*. Everything is okay." Elsa quietly reassured her.

Angelica opened her eyes and tried lifting her head, but it fell softly back onto the pillow. "It was the plague. All the fault of the plague."

"What plague, *Abuela*?"

"On the family hacienda, where the country house is at Wayi."

Angelica looked directly into Elsa's eyes. Elsa was impressed at her grandmother's awareness of time as she began to explain: "When I was little girl, before we fled to the capital, we lived on the hacienda. I have wonderful memories of life there: the river and the open fields resting below the mountains, and the kindness of the Indians. But that was before the darkness of the plague, before it swept over the land killing the crops and leaving the people trembling in fear." Angelica closed her eyes and clenched her bony hands in fists.

Elsa could see how upset Angelica was, so she calmed her by changing the subject.

"*Abuela,* tell me more about the beach outings with your kids. Those must have been good times." Angelica nodded her head, and fell back into a long sleep.

Later Elsa asked her father why he had never told her about the plague at the hacienda. He just shrugged and said, "I'm surprised my mother brought it up. She never liked to talk about it with us. It all happened so long ago and our family is sad enough as it is." Elsa figured her own troubles were just part of a long line of misfortunes in her family. The collapse of her dream of having a family was part of a greater web of loss, plagues, and death.

Angelica seemed to enjoy Elsa's visits, and would request that her granddaughter sit with her. Angelica would doze off, and Elsa would read or write in her journal quietly until her grandmother stirred.

"Elsa, look under the bed and you'll see a hatbox. Can you pull it out?" Angelica asked one afternoon.

Elsa got on her knees and crouched down, and saw a large, round box toward the foot of the bed. She reached and pulled it out. The tattered box was covered in dust, which Elsa wiped off slowly with tissues from the nightstand. As they sat together in the candle-lit room, Elsa opened the worn box and took out the remnants of bygone days. There were baby clothes—booties, jackets and caps—knitted in fine, shiny silk the color of gold.

Angelica explained to Elsa, "Before the plague, our family's silk was considered the most luxurious ever produced. My father exported the thread as far as China. The shiny golden hue was natural, never seen before in raw silk.

"My mother taught the Gomez Family, who still live in the country house, and now they are the only ones keeping the production going. If they stop, this lineage of silkworms will die forever."

"Why didn't anyone in our family keep it going, *Abuela*? What about your brother, Uncle José?"

"We all tried for a while. But life gets in the way, other obligations, and when my husband died, I was a widow raising my children alone. I do regret that we let it go," Angelica said wistfully. Then she added, "You might be the one to save it, my dear Elsita."

Elsa stroked her grandmother's arm and nodded her head in a reassuring manner, yet she knew that it was an impossible idea. She just didn't see the point in clarifying the matter with Angelica.

Elsa gently held the tiny Christening garments, so fine that the mere dryness of her skin snagged the thread. Then she reached into the box and felt something soft and round, the size of a quail egg. The cocoon was decades old, dried out but still intact, and when she held it up against the light of the candles, the silhouette of a dried pupa appeared like a curled shadowy embryo.

Chapter 2

Elsa had heard the family tales of Salvatore from her father ever since she was a child...

Salvatore had arrived in Peru from Italy, and ventured out into the Andes. He traveled by train, and sometimes by foot, alongside the Salkantay mountain range. The snow-capped jagged mountains rolled and snaked alongside Salvatore as he passed through arid valleys sheathed with long grasses. Quenual trees with twisty branches and golden-red fields of quinoa speckled the landscape.

He panned for gold in the Apurimac River, a violent river lined by the deepest canyons in the world. He was discouraged by his meager luck at finding gold; he hadn't calculated the voracity of the conquistadores in taking gold and silver out of that rich land. After a few months of mild success—a few small nuggets but not enough to build a fortune with—he realized he needed a new plan.

Salvatore eventually tired of wandering across the land, so when he stumbled upon the sunny valley of Acutambo he felt it was as good a place as any to settle.

With the savings he had left and with his father's help, he decided to buy land. He put his request in writing to the local magistrate. Salvatore stood outside the office waiting to meet with the civil officer. When they called him in, he bashfully sat down on a chair in the middle of the small, sparse room. Several curious officials wearing dingy chino uniforms watched the interview, leaning against the wall while scratching their bellies and picking at their teeth. They passed around his documents, and were obviously impressed by his Italian citizenship. As a foreigner, a European with white skin, he was more favorably looked upon as a landowner than the peasant Indians.

"You are so far from home. What brings you to our continent?" the official asked him as he examined Salvatore's passport.

"I was looking for gold," he stammered.

"Ah, *sí señor*, that is the eternal quest, is it not? And now that you see that all men were created equal in their delusions, are you sure you want to stay?"

Salvatore was too proud to go home in defeat. "I'd rather stay than face my mother."

The men laughed and scratched their bellies with more vigor.

After the brief interview, Salvatore bought a rather large piece of land, twenty-five hectares, for the equivalent cost of two cows, a goat, and five hens. Then he began construction of his house.

Hired workers dried red clay bricks in the sun, and made mortar out of the gray mud from the riverbank. They hiked into the foothills, collecting carizo reeds for the roofs. Crops of corn were planted, and the men built a mill, powered by one mule to grind sugarcane. They built a chapel and lodgings for the Indians who would work, marry, celebrate and die within the hacienda named Acutambo.

Salvatore knew the responsibility of housing workers, however the Quechua Indians were harder to understand than the boisterous Italians who sang and shouted and told jokes while they worked and drank wine and flirted with the women. The Indians tended to keep to themselves; they were quiet and reserved.

Salvatore knew silk production. It was a part of him, as if the fibers of his being were woven from those fine threads, and like tendons, held him together. His father had given him the silkworm eggs to get the business started, and in a letter to his father Salvatore said, "I think you would approve, and I promise to repay you someday. Thank you for your help, and give my regards to Mother."

Then Salvatore worked alongside his hired men as they cleared and tilled the land to plant mulberry trees and constructed sheds to house silkworms. Salvatore enjoyed the work: he transformed from a skinny, pale boy into a man.

And after a couple of years, he saw the fruits of his labor. While the men harvested in the fields and orchards, the Indian women gathered to weave. Others cared for the worms and moths spread on plank beds in various stages of the cycle.

Salvatore's encounters with the local, fiery mestizas were daunting. He was a good prospect, but he was timid. The women doubted his masculinity for his lack of machismo flair.

Don Emilio, el patrón from a nearby hacienda, brought his daughter, Lucía, to visit with Salvatore on a few occasions. The beautiful young girl had a soft, flowing figure and luxurious auburn hair, as well as piercing eyes and a proud chin. Salvatore found her beauty and confidence impressive, but he didn't quite know what to make of Lucía's chaperone. Her Aunt Esther always wore a long black frock and stood tall and rigid behind Lucía. She had pale skin, beady eyes, and her dark hair pulled back into a tight bun. She followed the two as Salvatore attempted a courtship.

He would scurry about self-consciously, asking the help to make his guests feel welcome. In the kitchen, the maids would say, "This is Don Salvatore's chance to make a good impression. Take out the lemonade on a tray and use the best dishes."

While Don Emilio napped on the veranda, Lucía and Salvatore walked through the silkworm sheds, with Esther following behind at a close distance. Lucía was fascinated with the worms. Esther clucked and shook her head with disapproval.

"These dank sheds are not fit for a lady. It stinks and the dampness will surely give Lucía a cold." Esther approached her niece, and tightened the shawl around Lucía's shoulders.

"Please, Auntie, I'm fine. I don't even need the shawl." Lucía freed herself from the grips of the wool. "But if you don't mind, I'm parched. Would you be so kind as to fetch me some water?" Lucía smiled sweetly at her aunt.

Esther stared back suspiciously, but quickly walked off toward the house. It was the first time Salvatore and Lucía were left alone together.

Salvatore tried to make small talk with sweat on his brow and a slight stutter. Lucía listened with patience. Finally, he gently took Lucía's hand into his own, and she didn't pull away. Instead, she stopped and leaned toward him with her eyes closed. Salvatore cleared his throat, took in a deep breath, and kissed her. The kiss was merely a peck, and yet as they walked back toward the house, so close that their arms touched, Salvatore was already planning the next kiss. As awkward as these encounters turned out, Salvatore was sure that Lucía was the one woman in the world who understood him.

It wasn't until after the wedding that Salvatore learned that Aunt Esther would be joining her niece on the hacienda. Salvatore never imagined that by marrying Lucía he would inherit this spinster aunt who had no place else to go, and who served no other purpose than playing nursemaid to her young niece.

During her first months at the hacienda, Esther was quiet and reserved. She watched with keen eyes the couple's inter-actions, as Salvatore scrambled to make Lucía comfortable. Esther happened to stand several inches above Salvatore. He would stammer, "Thank you, excuse me, please, I'm sorry," in a steady stream of distress. Esther merely smirked at his feeble attempts to assuage her. Her towering figure crept up behind him, stealthily and when he least expected it, and so he soon developed a nervous tic.

"You know, my niece could have married Leonardo, the judge's son. He courted her for a year," Esther told Salvatore during dinner one evening and intently watched his reaction. "Leonardo's family owns a summer home along the coast."

"That sounds nice," Salvatore replied.

"I have one piece of advice for you, Salvatore. You are a man now, and a husband, but you are weak and some might even consider you to be pathetic. My advice is to not be weak, or pathetic."

Salvatore knew she saw through him and sensed all of his weaknesses, and right then Salvatore decided he despised Aunt Esther.

Angelica's funeral drew the entire neighborhood into the San Martin Cathedral, only three blocks from her own home, where she had attended mass every Sunday for the last fifty years. White lilies surrounded her open casket. Elsa approached and peered inside. For the wake, Angelica had been dressed in a pale blue dress with matching eye shadow, her gray wisps of hair combed back neatly and her lips slightly turned up at the edges giving her a strange but serene smile.

Even though Elsa had known that Angelica was dying, it still didn't seem possible that she was gone. They had shared so many stories and conversations just days, even hours, ago. Elsa thought she was ready for her grandmother's death, but now Angelica seemed to be the only one that understood her pain; the only one who shared in her sense of loss. Tears ran down Elsa's face.

Elsa sheepishly made the sign of the cross over her chest while muttering the Lord's Prayer only because it seemed like the appropriate thing to do, and because these customs were bred into her like DNA. The Catholic faith seemed to Elsa more like a genetic imprint than a rational choice. She had fought it her whole life, but there it was in her time of grief, a response like a baby mimicking the sounds it hears without conscious effort, merely out of an instinct to connect to its own kind.

As Elsa stood and stared into the casket, the white lilies began to crawl and move over Angelica's body. The bright green stems stretched and grew, as they wound themselves around Angelica's arms and wrists, her legs and ankles. The trumpet shaped flowers bloomed brilliant and gigantic over her body, slowly draping and smothering her as if they were alive and intent to devour. Then the flowers began to ooze milky droplets, which gathered into puddles on the floor. Elsa's grief teemed and wound like the tearful lilies. She could hardly breathe, as if she herself were being smothered and devoured by heavy, tear-laden lilies, even as their sweet scent filled the air. Elsa tried to tell herself, this is only a vision of my sadness.

She stumbled away and sat down in the pew with her father and mother; Josephine had taken a red-eye and arrived at Lima that very morning. When Elsa sat down, Josephine held onto Elsa's hand and squeezed, placing it in her lap. Elsa glanced at her mother, noticing her gentle features, which always made

Elsa feel at peace. Next to them sat Aunt Lina, and they were surrounded by numerous extended family. The weeping was a requiem unto itself, and the plangent cries of one of her great-aunts reminded Elsa of a *llorona* hired for the funeral. She wasn't sure of her true relation with the woman because in Peru everyone was either an aunt or uncle or cousin. No one worried about distinctions like once or three times removed.

Elsa looked toward the casket once again, expecting to see the lilies teeming over her grandmother. The flowers were still.

They all listened to the monotonous, soothing homily of the priest. Elsa began to think about her conversations with Angelica, about the country house, the silkworm production and the Gomez family. Even the plague weighed on her, toying with her curiosity. What really happened at the hacienda? What might the place look like today? She wondered if anyone in the family ever visited the house. Her attention was brought back as the Mass ended and everyone stood up.

Leaving the church, Elsa walked alongside her parents. She glanced at her father, noticing how much he had aged in just a few days. She knew it was the stress of all of this, the sadness weighing on him. It was a shame, though typical, that her brother Alejandro skipped out on the funeral. He was always busy, a list of excuses with work and his own family keeping him distracted from any obligations with his parents. This often left Elsa feeling like an only child, and especially now that her parents were aging the burden of responsibility felt like hers alone.

Neighbors stood on the sidewalks in front of their colonial houses painted in rich hues of cobalt blue, mustard yellow, and brick red, and with ornate iron gates. They gave their condolences as the family passed by, patting Miguel on the shoulder affectionately and kissing Josephine on the cheek in commiseration. Miguel had known most of them since he was a child.

Many followed them into the house where Aunt Lina had set out finger food: empanadas filled with meat or spinach, sandwiches cut into perfect triangles, assorted sweets and pastries. People sat drinking tea or coffee while conversing solemnly.

Gradually the crowd dwindled, and Elsa sat at that familiar long table, where Angelica had served countless meals to loved ones. Elsa rubbed her hands along the worn, rough edge of the old wood. She remembered just then the sensation of her feet dangling, not yet reaching the floor and swinging under the table. The sensation of her elbows resting high above her waist. That table had seemed monolithic to her as a child.

Josephine strolled in and sat down next to Elsa. "Your father says that tomorrow we have to go to a lawyer's office for the reading of the will. The lawyer has asked for you to be there, too." Her mother rubbed at her temples and let out a sigh.

"He has asked me to be there? Isn't that strange?" Elsa wondered out loud.

"Angelica loved you very much. I'm sure you are in her will. That's not very strange."

"Yes, but she doesn't have many belongings." Elsa then thought her grandmother might have had some heirlooms, jewelry perhaps, though it wasn't like her to wear expensive jewelry.

Elsa took a moment to admire her mother's serenity, her calming aura, even with jetlag and the demanding events of the day. "When will you be going back to Missouri?" she asked.

"I'll be leaving in a couple of days with your father."

"You can't stay any longer?" Elsa didn't feel ready to head home to California. There wasn't anything waiting for her there– only the empty, lonely cabin. Even her teaching job was less secure, as she thought about her last meeting with the department chair. She was reminded of low enrollment and cutbacks at the college, and anyway, Charles was there. Elsa felt a rush of heat as she thought about how she used the far parking lot, dashing with her head down, and taking the back stairs to get to class. She hadn't mustered the courage, or the financial savings, to quit her job yet, though she thought about it daily. The only one there for her was her best friend Margot.

She imagined staying in Peru a few more weeks, and traveling some.

Josephine said, "You know, I have so many memories of this place."

"And of the country house, too?" Elsa asked her.

"That was a long time ago. You remember it, honey? You were so young the last time we were there, maybe five or six years old." Josephine looked up at the ceiling and closed her eyes.

"I remember some things, mostly great-grandmother Lucía. I remember the silkworms in the sheds out back. I remember Uncle José feeding them mulberry leaves. And I remember Lucía spinning thread." Elsa's mind drifted back.

"I didn't expect you to remember all of that, it was so long ago. But I'm glad that you do. It was a magical place and time." Josephine's voice trailed off.

The next morning, the family sat in an office in downtown Lima waiting for the attorney. The traffic from the busy street outside was a faint rumble in the background. The room was dim, yet sunlight from the single window casted pale-yellow rays across the wood floor. Elsa's eyes scanned the colonial, ornate room left lackluster by time and neglect. The wood floors gleamed, polished with wax, but the upholstery and wainscoting were faded and shabby. It had at one time been elegant, she imagined. Elsa had noticed the decay of poverty everywhere since her arrival. A thin layer of dust and grime coated the streets—the dry desert coastline never got rain to wash the city clean.

Her father slouched, and her mother stroked his hand gently. Her parents' bodies seemed to be folding in on themselves, out of fatigue and sadness. Elsa paced the room impatiently.

Her father adjusted his posture and sat upright. He took out a cigar from his shirt pocket, which he carried on him cut and ready to light. He used a lighter and puffed, turning the cigar in his mouth, over and over. Plumes of smoke swirled and the sweet acrid scent of tobacco began to overpower the space.

Aunt Lina, who had been sitting very still and quiet, complained to her brother, "Miguel, this doesn't seem like the right time to smoke."

"We've been waiting almost an hour, so I don't think a cigar is going to cause an uproar. I hardly think anyone cares," Miguel replied. He continued twirling the corona in his mouth, as if he were sucking candy from a stick.

"I agree with *Tia* Lina, *Papá*. It doesn't seem appropriate." Elsa tried coaxing him.

"*Ay, niñas.* Leave me in peace." He found a glass ashtray on the desk and scooted it closer to him.

The room was once again quiet, until Aunt Lina began to cry softly into a handkerchief. "What will I do now that our mother is gone?" she asked. Josephine went to Lina and placed her arm around her.

Elsa too felt grief, but somehow it became entwined with her own troubles over the past year, so that she could hardly tell which came first, sadness for Angelica's passing or sadness for her own loss.

In some ways, Elsa had found refuge in her pain and anger over the past year, as she used it as an excuse to avoid people and situations. Only while teaching did anxiety creep up, causing panic attacks that nearly made her run out of the classroom on several occasions. But mostly, for the first few months after her divorce, she had felt empty and detached. That feeling of detachment scared her more than the anxiety. Detachment meant a loss of her passion for life, and the emptiness had felt engulfing. The day she caught Charles in the parking lot, kissing the girl, she had driven away in her car without confronting them. She still regretted that, taking the cowardly way out. Sometimes she relived that moment over in her imagination, and she walked right up to them, not allowing Charles the easy way out.

Now Elsa watched the smoke from the cigar, the white puffs rising higher, swirling in wispy clouds. When her eyes reached the ceiling, she took in a quick breath and clutched the armrests of her chair. She was mesmerized as she watched the billowing figure of Angelica form out of the smoke. The hazy image of her grandmother hovered benignly in the beams overhead.

Elsa felt herself being pulled and drifting away.

Suddenly the attorney strolled in, unapologetic and serious. Elsa was brought back to the moment, and the room felt cold and dark. She shook off the feeling of Angelica's presence and focused on the young man. She was surprised by his rigid manner, as he reached out his hand and curtly greeted the grieving family.

"Buenas tardes, mi nombre es José Rodriguez."

Elsa took notice of his suit, pressed and clean, but nearly frayed at the seams and one size too small. His black shoes were scuffed. Even attorneys suffered the pervasive poverty of the country.

He continued, "I will be reading the last will and testament of Señora Angelica Rosa Santos de Léon. We will begin now." With an authoritative tone, he began reading from the document.

Though not a wealthy woman, and having been widowed decades before, Angelica had owned her home. Everyone knew the house in Lima would be bequeathed to Aunt Lina.

As José read, Elsa's attention once again was drawn to the beams overhead. She could barely see Angelica, her smoky figure faded into the dark corners.

Elsa looked to her father, who was starting to raise his voice at the attorney, "What do you mean the country house? We haven't been there in years. I didn't even know my mother still owned the place."

"Yes, sir. It says plainly right here. The property located in Wayi, in the Abancay Province of the Apurimac Region, is hereby bequeathed to Señora Elsa Maria Léon Peters." He went on also to name her brother Alejandro as co-heir to the country house.

Elsa couldn't quite register the information that the old country house, the place where a small silkworm industry once thrived, was now hers and her brother's. Briefly she fixated on the fact that the document contained her married name Peters.

Her father, in confusion, continued his protest to the attorney. "How is this possible? I thought the house had been sold already."

"And Miguel's children can't possibly keep the place," Aunt Lina chimed in.

"Why not?" Elsa asked. She hadn't expected this reaction, though she herself was still stunned by the news.

"Well, for one thing, it's too dangerous in the Andes," her father explained.

Elsa felt that strange pull once again, and glanced up at the beams. The smoke lingered there, and out of the haze her grandmother floated and swayed gently. Elsa sensed once again that pull, as the billowing form seemed to appear through some passageway of mist and twinkling lights.

Elsa shuddered and asked, "Do you see that, Mom?"

Josephine had been quiet throughout the discussion, understanding that the will was her husband's affair. Josephine was American and she had little say in these legal matters. Now she answered her daughter. "I have to say that I agree with your father, it's too dangerous for you to even think about visiting the place."

"But do you see that?" Elsa pointed up toward the beams.

Josephine looked up and asked, "What is it, sweetie? Are you feeling okay, you're looking very pale." Her mother rose and walked over the Elsa, placing her hand on her daughter's forehead.

Elsa watched her grandmother fade away, leaving only cobwebs and dust particles floating in the dim light.

Her father stared at Elsa blankly then shook his head. "Nothing good can come of this. We have to sell that house."

"Yes, I agree. The house has to be sold," Aunt Lina added.

"We can certainly arrange that," José offered and began to rise from the desk. "If both parties agree to it, we can draw up the documents for a sale."

"I'm sure Alejandro will want to sell," Miguel said.

"Wait, I don't understand. Why are you pushing for this so quickly? I just get the news that we've inherited a house, and you don't even give me a chance to breathe. Please, everyone stop." Elsa was now flushed and pacing the small office. She remembered Angelica's stories about the country house, and her suggestions about Elsa saving the silkworm lineage.

Elsa faced her family. "Tell me the truth. Why are you so eager to get rid of the house? I know there's something you're not saying."

Her father and Aunt Lina looked at each other, neither offering an explanation.

Elsa persisted, "What happened there? Does this have any-thing to do with the plague?" Waiting for a reply, she folded her arms.

Aunt Lina looked surprised. Then she sighed heavily and took one more glance at her brother, and began, "Elsa, there was a murder at the hacienda."

"A murder?" Elsa was stunned. Why didn't Angelica tell her? Elsa was hurt that her grandmother kept that startling piece of information from her.

Lina continued to explain, "My mother never liked to speak of it. She was afraid it would curse us. As she became senile, I'm not even sure she let herself remember it at all."

Miguel approached Elsa, placing his hands on her shoulders. Elsa could see the pain in his eyes, as he told her, "My grandmother, Lucía, fled from that house many years ago, saying that it was haunted. Of course, none of us believed her, and anyway she was very old by then. But when she finally told us about her Aunt Esther, who was murdered in the house, we had it verified. Lucía was just a young woman at the time, married and raising her children–Uncle José and our mother Angelica."

Miguel walked over to a chair and sat down. He continued, "My brother and I traveled there after Lucía passed on, and we learned about the murder from some of the Indians who had worked on the hacienda. Our grandmother's aunt had been killed in the house, and they suspected one of the Indians."

"But there was never any proof that he did it," Aunt Lina added.

Miguel paused and held his head in his hands. He was clearly upset by sharing this with his daughter. The turmoil of his family was stirred–these were things he probably didn't want known or he would have shared it with Elsa before this. Now he continued, "I knew there was something wrong there–my mother even took a priest once, but he wouldn't stay. A murder leaves evil in its wake."

"I remember going there as a child, *Papá*."

"Yes, but after Lucía died it was different. We never went back after that."

Elsa was surprised to hear her father talk of ghosts and evil. She could see her father was distraught and how worried Aunt Lina was. Elsa tried to understand what all of this meant to her, and meant for her inheritance.

Generations had lived on the land, loved it and nurtured it. Salvatore traveled across oceans for it, built the hacienda and established a small, yet thriving silkworm industry. Lucía wove garments from the silk produced by the worms, and taught the local Indians how to keep the production alive. Lucía raised her children, Angelica and José, on those sloping hillsides surrounded by mountain peaks, abundant in fruits and flowing rivers.

Then Angelica gave this small remnant, what was left of the hacienda, to her grandchildren who hardly knew her at all. Elsa wanted to see the house.

"*Papá*, I want to go. The house belongs to Alejandro and to me, so I have the right to see it and decide what to do with it." Elsa sat back down in a chair. She brushed a strand of hair from her face, and then tied her long locks up into a loose bun. Feeling angry and rebellious, her face flushed a bright pink.

"Well, I guess we have no say in the matter," her mother replied. "You are a grown woman. You've certainly always had a mind of your own."

"Well, you can thank *Abuelita*. This wasn't my idea," Elsa reminded her parents.

"*Hermano*, the Gomez Family is still there taking care of the place," Aunt Lina said. "They're a nice family."

Elsa remembered then what Angelica had told her about the Gomez Family: they were the last ones keeping the silk production going in the Andes–the golden silk that shimmered.

"But Elsa can't possibly make the trip there," her father said sternly. "It's too remote. And times aren't the same. That's a dangerous area now–it was a red zone not long ago."

Elsa knew her father referred to *Sendero Luminoso*, Shining Path, as well as the MRTA. Both terrorist groups had been dismantled with the capture of their leaders, but rogue members still roamed the Andes, as well as thieves who worked in gangs, targeting tourists. She had seen stories in the news of buses being hijacked and *gringos* being kidnapped for ransom. But Elsa believed those incidents were rare, and usually hyped up by the media. She figured that her father was just being overprotective. He had always been that way.

Elsa's mind was whirling. She had inherited a country house in a remote, dangerous area of the Andes. A house where a murder had taken place and was left haunted? It all seemed unreal, but it couldn't possibly be as crazy as it sounded. There had to be some logic to all of this.

"I have to go, *Papá*. I hope you understand. I need this." Elsa felt a swell of emotion rise up, and she was relieved to be feeling again. Her fear of that engulfing emptiness subsided, as tears filled her eyes. "I need this," she said again, this time to her mom.

"We know you've been through a lot, honey. We told you to give it time, and you'd bounce back," her mother said as she stroked Elsa's shoulder. Elsa believed that her parents were relieved to have Charles out of their lives. Family gatherings had been tense, as Charles was often unbearably pretentious. He grew up in the San Fernando Valley, but had cultivated a quasi-British accent. Elsa would cringe at that behavior now, but at the time she had defended him blindly.

But she knew her parents grieved the miscarriages along with her wholeheartedly. Elsa had two losses in a three-year period. They had all wondered if that's what spurred Charles's affair.

"We're tired. Let's talk about this at home." Miguel seemed to have run out of steam.

They were exhausted from the events of the last few days, the funeral and endless stream of visitors paying their respects, and now this sudden news. They walked out of the building and onto the busy city street.

Chapter 3

Arriving at the house, Elsa called her brother with the news. "We inherited the country house in the Andes. Did you know about the property, Alex?" she asked. She twirled the plastic cord of the phone as she spoke.

"Sounds like it's in the middle of fucking nowhere. What are we supposed to do with it? Hey, how much do you think it's worth?" That was her brother, always looking to make a buck and as unsentimental as they come.

"Honestly, I'm sure it's worthless. But I'm visiting the place to check it out. I'll let you know more after I see it." Elsa felt like crying out to her brother, it's not about money, it's about our family and our history. She kept the sentiment to herself, knowing that her brother didn't feel a connection to Peru.

"We can't just leave the house abandoned, can we?" Alejandro asked.

"There's a family of caretakers who have lived there for many years, so it's not abandoned. But I don't know what condition I'll find it in. I'll let you know more when I get back."

"Okay, let me know."

Elsa looked down at the old rotary phone, with its plastic dial and faded case. She enjoyed the weight of the receiver in her hand—it felt solid and comforting.

The next day, Elsa heard Aunt Lina call out to her from down the hallway, "Elsita, I'm stepping out for a minute, why don't you come with me?" Aunt Lina was going out to buy fresh bread.

"Okay, *Tia,* I'll be right there."

Her aunt was a gentle, passive presence who ensured the smooth functioning of that big house, giving the illusion that the house itself anticipated the needs of its inhabitants. There was always hot tea in the thermos and warm rolls in the basket on the table every morning. Every day there were fresh towels in the bathroom and the laundry was hung on the cord in the back porch to soak in the meager sun and then was prudently taken down before the damp night descended. It was easy to forget that someone was responsible for the care of such mundane matters.

Maria, the maid, came every other day and she was hard to miss. Loud and energetic, she sang while she dusted and often yelled at the dog while chasing him down the hall with a rolled up newspaper. But one day, as Elsa caught sight of Lina taking clothes off the line and placing them in a basket for Maria to then iron out their stiffness, it dawned on her that it was an immense amount of work to keep up such a large house.

Now as they walked to the corner, Lina leaned in close and spoke sternly to Elsa. "My dear, I am very fond of you, so I have to tell you that I'm worried. I don't think you realize how dangerous it is to be a woman traveling alone through the Andes. It's dangerous for anyone really, with those bandits on the roads. If you were staying on the tourist track, and visiting Machu Picchu, it would be fine, but the country house is very remote."

"I don't see how I even have a choice, since I inherited the place. We can't just leave it forever," Elsa responded. "Besides, I want to go. I'm not afraid."

"I heard that the Gomez family is still making silk, though it doesn't seem to have much to do with us anymore," Lina said under her breath.

They approached an old cart with an elderly man slowly pushing it along, and Lina ordered ten rolls from the baker, paying him in coins. As they turned back toward the house, Elsa helped Lina avoid a crack in the cement, where she had nearly missed a step and stumbled.

"Then this is what we have to do. I have a friend who works at a travel agency in Cuzco. I'll call her to set you up with a driver, like an escort, someone trustworthy and who knows the area well. How does that sound?" Lina offered.

As they approached the front door and Lina took out her key, Elsa agreed to the arrangement. Part of her was relieved because she had felt nervous about making the trip alone, though she never would have admitted it to her family. She was tired of being the victim. She wanted to prove to them that she was strong and capable, but now this seemed to be a reasonable compromise.

Elsa thought about her wedding ring. She had packed it in her jewelry bag, just in case. She didn't want to wear it in front of her parents, but she had secretly worried about traveling as a single woman in Peru. She knew the men could be aggressive, and she didn't have the confidence or practice to manage advances. Now she imagined the ring coming in handy.

Elsa found her parents sitting at the table, drinking morning coffee Peruvian style: instant Nescafé with canned evaporated milk. Miguel sat close to Josephine, and Elsa took note that he hadn't left her side since the funeral. He seemed attached to his wife, as if she were an anchor and he was in a raging storm at sea.

"Here are rolls to go with our coffee," Aunt Lina said as she passed the bread basket to Josephine.

Elsa bit into a warm bun and smiled at the soft delicious-ness. Elsa told her mom, "I spoke to Margot yesterday. She sends her condolences to the family."

Margot was like the sister that Elsa never had. They had been best friends since college, and had seen many of life's ups and downs together: marriages, divorce, birth and miscarriages.

"That's good to know, dear," Josephine said. "How is her son doing?"

"Kyle's starting college this fall, so Margot is thrilled for him. Though she's a bit of a wreck to see him go."

"And her bookstore?" Josephine asked.

"Slow as always, but she hangs in there."

Elsa loved the little bookstore. It was one of those charming stores that sold rare, out-of-print books shelved around wood-work and natural light.

Miguel just nodded his head in silence.

Josephine then asked, "Are you sure you won't come back with us, Elsa?"

"I have to see the house before deciding to sell it or not." Elsa held firm, though she knew her parents wouldn't rest until they knew she was back in Lima. And she still wondered about the mysteries the house held.

"Ay, I don't want to listen to this rubbish. You are being too stubborn about this, *mi hija*." Her father rose from the table agitated.

"This is not my fault, *Papá*. This was Angelica's idea, not mine. So it's not fair that you're being so hard."

"She wasn't thinking clearly. I should have the will annulled."

"*Papá*, listen to me. Why do you think Angelica would want me to go there? Why would she have chosen me?" Elsa had been asking herself that question.

"I have no idea why she would do this."

"I think that you do, *Papá.*" Elsa trembled with emotion.

Her father sank down into his chair. He looked down at his feet, suddenly defeated and tired.

"Maybe I'm the only one with nothing to lose." Elsa's eyes filled with tears. "I have nothing to lose, so let me do it."

Miguel rested his head in his hands. "We do have a lot to lose. We don't want to lose you, Elsa."

"You have to trust me, *Papá.* I'm not a child," Elsa said as she placed her arm around her father's shoulder.

"How long will you stay there?" her mother asked.

"I don't have to be back until mid-August, so maybe three weeks, or a month. It might depend on how I find things," Elsa explained. She didn't feel any rush to get back.

"Well, keep us posted on your plans. And look after yourself, sweetie," her mother said tenderly.

"I promise I will, Mom."

"I still don't approve, *Hija,*" her father mumbled.

"Aunt Lina is getting me a driver, an escort. So you don't need to worry, *Papá.*"

"That's something but perhaps not enough, I'm afraid." He exhaled deeply.

When they heard a honk from outside and the dog barking, they all got up and made their way down the hallway. Elsa and her parents watched as the taxi was loaded with suitcases. Aunt Lina made the sign of the cross on Miguel and Josephine's foreheads, as she said, "*Vayan con Dios.*"

"*Mi hija,* be careful on the road. I will be praying for you," Miguel told his daughter.

Elsa became lost in thought, as she watched the taxi drive down the street and out of sight. Elsa had felt like she was drowning in deep waters, with weights pulling her down: the weight of job insecurity, the weight of divorce, and the unbearable weight of her lost hope for motherhood, which was the hardest to accept. Now she felt that she was reaching for the surface with all her might, breaking through the water and gasping for breath. The breath was painful and sharp, but there was great relief in the feeling of survival.

Feeling nervous about the condition of the house and what she might find there, Elsa was still filled with excitement. She told herself to take things one-step at a time. She would fly into Cuzco, and then travel by car through the Sacred Valley to Wayi, where the house sat waiting.

Arriving in Cuzco, Elsa felt lightheaded and short-of-breath from the altitude, and yet the crisp, cool mountain air was invigorating. The city was exciting and so different, with its layers of culture and strange beauty, and it was one of Elsa's favorite places to visit. The last time she was there, it was with Charles. After staying at the old house in Lima for several days, they had traveled around the country, visiting the main tourist sights of Machu Picchu and the Nazca Lines along the southern coast. It felt strange to be walking the streets alone now.

Elsa allotted a two-day stay while Paco, her escort, arranged his schedule to take her to Wayi. She would pay him thirty dollars a day, plus food, lodging and gas. It seemed like a good deal to Elsa.

The first day, Elsa explored with curiosity and energy, but she also found herself melancholic. She wasn't sure if her mood was shaped by that feeling which overcomes someone after passing too much time alone in public places, where jovial groups chatted together at large tables and lovers held hands in dim, cozy tables for two. She sat writing in her journal and watching strangers pass by.

As Elsa sat at a small table facing the plaza, she twirled her wedding ring around. It had already come in handy when she checked in at the hotel, and an overly assertive man standing next to her at the counter insisted on making small talk, until she casually mentioned her husband. He backed off immediately. Now she rubbed at the gold band, wishing she didn't have to make this trip alone. Everything seemed harder.

Elsa continued twisting the ring, as she thought back to her trip with Charles. She avoided the café at the other side of the plaza, where they had eaten a couple of times. She remembered the fight they had over the street vendors. Charles was annoyed and rude to the young artists trying to sell their drawings. Elsa knew the kids were pushy and overcharging the tourists, but still, she sympathized with their struggles. Charles brushed them away with irritation. Then Elsa's mind drifted to their excursion along the southern coast to the Nazca desert.

They had walked through a pre-Inca, Indian cemetery of barren desert with broken pottery, pieces of textiles and fragments of bones scattering the rocky, dry terrain. It was interminable flat land weathered by winds, blowing sand across the expanse. Elsa had tied a scarf around her head and covered her face to keep the sand from her eyes.

They knelt at gravesites, picking through the meager remains—what was left by tomb raiders decades ago. She found an interesting piece of pottery: a portion of a jar with a black painted geometric design. Elsa put the ceramic in her pocket, planning to sneak it through Customs on her way home. Charles poked at some bones. They each seemed lost in their own world, miles apart from each other, as they roamed the desert.

That night, in a small seaside hostel in Paracas, Elsa had come down with a fever. She rested on the musty bed in a fitful state with chills, nausea and a headache, mulling over the cleanliness of the restaurants they had eaten at that day. Charles kept a cool washcloth on her forehead, and found a pharmacy and bought medicine. He stayed up with her all night. While he nursed her, Elsa felt closer to Charles.

Now Elsa imagined getting sick, alone, and though she knew she could take care of herself, still the thought unsettled her.

Elsa left the café and began walking. She felt bewitched by the constant gray that washed over everything with a somber shade. Cuzco was a city of stone, and the maze of rock walls, perfectly assembled and aligned, attracted tourists from all over the world. Below the walls ran rustic cobblestone streets, winding narrowly throughout the city, also in every shade of gray.

Elsa began to work her way through the narrow, steep streets at San Blas, and a street kid tagged alongside her.

"Hey *Señorita*, I give you tour for ten soles. Por favor, you want tour, my English is good." He was a bright-eyed boy who had learned to act professionally. He looked Elsa in the eyes and shook her hand.

"Yes, your English is very good. Okay, walk with me." She was happy to have the company. Other street children gathered around and walked along behind them.

He was able to explain in broken English what Elsa already knew of that mysterious land.

"There is a legend…" the boy said.

He told her about how the Inca Empire was founded, in that allegorical belly-button of the world, by its very first king, Manco Capac, believed to be the offspring of a luminous, warm father: the Sun. This mystical incarnation of a king rose up out of the middle of Lake Titicaca along with his bride in hand, Mama Ocllo.

The city Cuzco was conquered by Francisco Pizarro and his men, riding into the city on tall, hoofed beasts with fierce dogs by their sides. Dressed in steel armor from head to toe, what a sight the conquistadores must have been, frightening and prophetic.

Now along the ancient Inca walls rose Spanish colonial stucco buildings with ornate balconies trimmed with carved wood and painted in deep, rich colors.

The plaza was buzzing, and it seemed eerily paradoxical. There was color everywhere, the Indians with brilliant hues woven into their full skirts and ponchos, and tapestries strewn throughout store shop doorways. Yet the gray tones of the rock walls and cobblestone streets glistened, covering everything in a shimmering light of silver so that the city, although bright, was seemingly drenched with wet tears.

"Your tour was first-rate, and here's a tip," she told the boy. Elsa's imagination reeled with fantastical images of conquistadores and Inca kings.

"*Gracias Señorita*, you come back tomorrow and I show you the ruins on the hill," he said as he scampered off with a trail of kids in his wake.

The Spanish cathedral presided over the plaza, large and impressive. Elsa felt drawn to it. She was thinking about Angelica's funeral. Even though she wasn't religious, she still had to believe in the magic of life and the possibility of divine intervention. And she still felt the awe and peace from the candles, incense, chants, and the art inside the church. Despite knowing the historical brutality of the Catholic Church, she couldn't help the feeling of reverence.

Elsa sat in a pew, glancing around at the paintings and statues along the walls in the dim, candlelit nave. She took in a deep breath, and as she exhaled she tried to release the knot in her chest. She tried to relax her entire being. She willed herself to let go of the tension and fear knotted at her core. Elsa closed her eyes and prayed to a benevolent, loving force. Please let me find peace; please help me let go of anger. I want to love again. Elsa left the cathedral feeling hopeful.

Outside in the plaza, young backpackers with long tangled hair, wearing handcrafted garments, roamed the streets. Cars tooted their horns at the crossing llamas and children. The city was rustic, indigenous, and ancient, and yet strangely cosmopolitan. Hip, modern nightclubs and fine restaurants overflowed with foreigners, while locals sold monstrous corn on the cob, grown in the Sacred Valley, so named for the immensity of the corn kernels produced out of its rich soils.

Elsa approached a stout woman sitting beside a large cauldron on the street corner. With dirt-caked hands, she wrapped an ear in some husks, and grabbed a chunk of goat cheese, tucking it inside. She handed it to Elsa, and Elsa bit into the cob. Anywhere else it might have seemed unappetizing, but here it was a delicacy.

The next day, Elsa called Margot from her cell phone. Normally, Elsa tried to avoid using her phone while traveling, but she needed to hear her friend's voice. She felt relief and comfort wash over her when Margot answered, "Hey there, darling. So where has this Peruvian adventure taken you now?"

"I'm in Cuzco, Margot. We have to come here together some day. You'd love it. It's very exotic. I'm on my way to the country house. I decided that I just had to see it for myself," Elsa explained.

"Of course you need to see it, honey."

"My father didn't think so. My family put up quite the fight. You know, a woman traveling alone, and all." Elsa felt out-of-breath and excited as she told Margot about the murder at the hacienda and the haunting.

Margot's response, after hearing about the history of the house and Elsa's decision to stay a few weeks, was not exactly what Elsa had expected from her free-spirited best friend. "Elsa, maybe your parents were right. It does sound odd, don't you think?"

"You don't really believe the house is haunted, Margot? Do you?"

"I'm just saying, it doesn't sound right. The story about the house seems creepy. And you don't know this driver, the chaperone. How can you be sure it's safe?"

"I'm surprised, Margot. I thought you were going to suggest a séance, or some kind of ritual in honor of the ghosts." Elsa felt that something was wrong with her friend. She didn't hear the support and sense of humor that she was used to with Margot.

"Hell, what do I know about it? Maybe I'm just envious of your adventures. I haven't been feeling myself lately," Margot stated flatly.

"Is something wrong, Margot?" Elsa asked.

"Kyle is moving away soon for college, so I think that has me feeling blue." Margot reassured Elsa.

Elsa had always counted on Margot to appreciate the magic of life. She rarely judged and more often supported Elsa's decisions. This change in Margot's attitude threw Elsa off, made her doubt carrying through with her plan. She made her way down the street from her hotel to the meeting spot with her driver feeling reluctant and nervous, rolling her suitcase behind her.

Elsa was expecting Paco to pick her up that afternoon. She waited for him at the Monastery, as she explored the serene grounds and sat in the garden drinking herbal hot tea made from the leaves of the coca plant.

The Indians used coca leaves for centuries to boost their energy and alleviate their hunger pains. They tucked a ball of leaves into their cheek, much like a wad of chewing tobacco. Coca tea was offered in the airport and in all of the hotels to soothe tourists from the shock of the altitude.

The Monastery had a chapel, a small room frosted with silver and gold dripping from ornately carved wood. Far from whimsical and fair, like Renaissance cherubs floating in clouds laced with golden light and pale blue skies, the paintings in this chapel were dark and ominous as fearful mortals bearing clubs and swords fought off demons with antlers and dragon tails. Many of the paintings were in tones of dark red and burgundy, the colors of blood, wine, and devils.

Contrasting with the chapel, the courtyard was light and cheery. Flowerbeds overflowed with roses burgeoning in shades of peach and pink, with elegant tables set under a centenarian Pisonay tree.

Elsa walked out to the plaza with her bags, at the set meeting time. A beat-up Toyota pulled up and the driver waved at her, as she was the only *gringa* with luggage standing on the corner. Elsa leaned into the passenger side. "*Hola, Paco.* My name is Elsa. *Mucho gusto.*" She climbed into the back seat, while Paco got out and put her bags in the trunk.

"*Buenas tardes, señorita.* Looks like you're all ready to go. Would you like to stop at the ruins on the hill before we leave the city? It will only take a couple of hours," Paco suggested. Their conversation continued in a slow, polite Spanish. Elsa had been improving and becoming more fluent with each passing day. It usually took her some time and practice to regain vocabulary and verb conjugations, but by now she felt at ease and confident with the language.

Elsa agreed that a visit to the Sacsaywaman ruins was worth the time. As they wound their way up in the battered car along the precariously narrow road, Paco shared not only history about the city, but also some views on politics–mostly about the rampant corruption and poverty. He was an older man, Elsa guessed in his late sixties, heavy-set and ruddy, and he tended to sweat when he talked.

"How is it you know so much history, Paco?" Elsa asked, curious about him.

"I moved to Cuzco from Lima, where I was an agrarian professor at the National University. These are the conditions in my country–I make more money as a driver than as a professor. Anyway, this is a good retirement."

This reminded Elsa once again of her own teaching job and the meeting about cutbacks.

For now, she decided to put worries about job security out of her mind for the trip, though she put herself on a tight budget. In times past, Elsa would work at Margot's bookstore to make a little extra money. But she knew that it was getting harder for Margot to hire help. Now, every dollar spent added to Elsa's perceived deficit.

Though Paco talked a lot, he was full of good advice. He warned Elsa not to over tip, and explained how to barter in the shops.

When they arrived at the ruins, Paco said, "I'll be your guide, and that way we can avoid the crowds."

After their afternoon sojourn at the ruins, which he explained in great detail as they walked together, he suggested they drive to Pisac in the Sacred Valley, en route to Machu Picchu. Normally, tourists took the train to Machu Picchu, skipping altogether the quaint villages speckling the valley and the myriad of ruins.

As they got to know each other, Elsa was glad to have Paco's company during her otherwise solitary journey. He was agreeable and trustworthy, with a true passion for life leaning toward over-exuberance. She soon discovered his uncommon obsession and intrigue with the Virgin Mary and Old Western movies. On both subjects he had limitless knowledge and shared boundless trivia.

"This country ain't big enough for the two of us—I'm giving you 'til sundown to get out of town." Paco quoted the line from Walter Houston in *The Virginian*, without any natural inflection. He must have memorized it by rote, for he barely spoke a word of English otherwise. Elsa was surprised and laughed out loud.

"You do that, and I'll kill ya," Paco said with a big, goofy grin. "John Wayne," he said nodding to himself. He talked about the movies *Shane, True Grit, The Good, the Bad, and the Ugly,* and how he knew all about the actors and directors and where the movies were filmed and in what year, was a mystery to her.

The next day, while sitting in a small courtyard at a rustic hostel in Ollantaytambo, the last town en route to Aguas Calientes, which rested just below Machu Picchu, Elsa wrote in her journal. She wanted to remember the details of this trip. Elsa paused and gazed up into the rugged hillsides draped with lush foliage. She thought about her grandmother. Angelica had destined Elsa to make this journey, and Elsa felt Angelica's spirit quietly accompany her—urging her forward.

Chapter 4

A couple of days later, Elsa and Paco drove along even more remote roads towards the family's old house, which at one time was a part of the hacienda. As they drove alongside a jagged landscape, Paco pointed up toward a deep crevice carved into a mountainside. He leaned his whole body forward so he could see out the grimy front window. "Do you see that barren patch in the mountain?"

The large, gray gash ran from the top of the green mountain down to the river, which they were now passing through. The car was driving off the road straight into the shallow river, and the water almost reached the fenders. They crossed slowly and were met on the other side by the continuing dirt road, as if the river were just a natural extension of the roadway.

"There used to be a town up there, actually not so much a town as a small village. A few years ago, as the people were sleeping in the middle of night, a mudslide washed down from the top of the mountain and buried the entire village, almost two hundred souls. It came down so sudden and quickly, probably most of them didn't wake up before they were buried alive. But I imagine that the landslide carrying mud, water and debris would be accompanied by a tremendous roar, so maybe some had woken up just seconds before," Paco explained as Elsa shuddered.

"Now you see that little house right at the foot of the hillside?" Just next to the gray gash on the mountainside there was a small dwelling barely visible from the road.

"It is said that the night before the mudslide, an old, lone shepherd was walking through the village. He knocked on one door to ask for shelter and food for the night, but he was turned away. He went to another home and asked for a meal and lodging, but they also turned him away. He knocked at the door of every house in the village and was turned away by them all, until he reached that little house." Paco pointed with added emphasis at the house in the distance.

"The people in that home took in the old, tired man. They invited him to sit at their humble table and eat with them. They served him hot soup with potatoes and coca tea. They gave him a place to sleep with warm blankets and the stove burning nearby, and in the morning they sent him off with kind words."

"The very next night, the mudslide tore down the mountain and engulfed the town, and destroyed every single house except for that one."

Paco paused for dramatic effect. "They say that the little old man was actually Jesus, and he was testing the townspeople's kindness. Since then, many Indians claim to be visited by an old, lone shepherd and most of them are reluctant to turn him away."

"Are you telling me that people believe Jesus walks around these mountains to test them, and that if someone should fail his test it's punishable by a horrible and sudden death?" Elsa was incredulous. "I don't think Jesus would be setting a very good example of loving compassion and forgiveness by playing such a cruel trick on the people, do you?" she asked, annoyed at the harsh legend.

"The locals don't see it that lway. Anyway, it's probably for the best that they're a little scared–it will make them nicer to each other."

Paco's story made Elsa more aware of venturing into the culture, where the rules and mores of life were largely unknown to her. Even though her family was Peruvian, she would be viewed as a foreigner in the Andes. This made her vulnerable, as she considered the formidable nature surrounding them, and the reserved nature of the Indians.

Elsa was starting to get used to Paco's strange folklore and declarations of sightings and visions of Jesus and the Virgin Mary. They seemed to be all around, their figures surrounding them in those mountains–etched into the rugged earth. And anyway, how could she judge him for that? She had her own visions of Angelica floating in beams and reaching out to her. Of her tormented great-grandfather, Salvatore, crying out to his beloved Lucía. She was on her way to a house haunted by ghosts.

A short time passed. "There he is, look carefully," Paco said.

He was once again pointing with his finger up at a mountainside. "That is the figure of Juan Diego."

Elsa couldn't help but wonder what an image of the Mexican campesino, the shepherd to whom the vision of the Virgin de Guadalupe appeared, would be doing all the way in the Andes.

"Can you see him there, on his knees, reaching up with his arms toward the sky?"

She peered into the mountain, and into the rocky slopes with crevices and shadows creating the image, an apparition for believers. Elsa had to admit to Paco that she could make out the image of a man kneeling.

All the figures Paco saw in the mountains were angels, saints, or virgins. So many figures looming over him in that grandiose nature, Elsa knew it must give him great comfort. Could she find comfort in them, too? The further into the mountains they drove, the more Elsa struggled to let go of the past, of clinging memories that had kept her awake most nights. Charles and his lover still followed her, but she felt herself pushing them away. The grief that was her constant companion since her two miscarriages, since Charles abandoned her in the midst of her pain, was looking her straight in the face, asking her to confront its power over her.

Elsa and Paco were passing alongside open fields emitting the strong scent of anise. It smelled like sweet black licorice for miles around. The terraced hillsides were every shade of earthy colors. Crops of corn, quinoa, potatoes and beans made patchwork designs along the hills, while snow-capped peaks sat in the distance. Elsa saw a wild herd of vicuña run across a sloping field of long, dry grasses.

"Look, Paco."

"Oh, my country is very beautiful," he said with a sigh.

As they turned a corner, ahead in the distance Elsa could see several figures standing in the middle of the road. Paco didn't say anything, but she noticed that he slowed down the car and scooted himself upright. Even by his profile, she could see his face harden into a grimace. "Damn it," he cursed under his breath. With one hand on the steering wheel, he used the other to pull out his wallet. He put his ID card on the dashboard.

When they got closer, Elsa saw several men dressed in fatigues carrying machine guns. She wasn't sure if they were government, because even rebels wore military looking garb. There was a concrete blockade on the dirt road. She felt a surge of fear, a terror gripping her gut. Her father's voice rushed back to her, all of his lecturing and concerns. Why hadn't she listened to him?

Paco told her, "Quiet. Don't say a word." They approached but stopped a short distance from the blockade. Elsa glanced around and there were no other cars in sight.

A skinny man, wearing baggy fatigues and with a machine gun dangling heavily off his shoulder, jogged up to the driver's side. Paco rolled down the window and said, "*Buenos dias, jefe. Is there any problem here?*" He handed over his documentation.

The man looked over at Elsa, staring at her intently. She noticed the other men became curious, and slowly began to approach the car.

"May I get out of the car, *jefe*? We can talk, no?" Paco was sweating profusely; his dress shirt was stained with dark patches. But his voice sounded upbeat. The man looked down at Paco's ID and nodded.

Elsa watched nervously as Paco stood outside the car and chatted with the man, while others gathered around casually, with their weapons hung at their sides. Elsa's heart was beating hard and fast in her chest, and she could barely breathe. The air felt heavy and oppressive. Thoughts of her father still ran through her mind, how worried he had been, how stubborn and selfish she was.

Gradually there was a change in the atmosphere outside, as Elsa saw the men start to laugh. They were now all standing in a circle, and Paco was talking loudly and animated, gesturing wildly with his hands and arms. The men slapped their knees and doubled over with laughter. The skinny man grabbed at Paco's shoulder, pushing him playfully.

Paco skipped up to the car and leaned in, his arms resting on the door. "*Todo está bien, mi niña.*" His face was beet red, but he wore a big smile.

"What happened?" Elsa was in shock.

"It turns out that I know the boy's uncle. We went to school together. Unfortunately, we are going to still have to give them money. They prefer American dollars to soles– a twenty should be enough."

Elsa rifled through her backpack and pulled out a small coin purse. Her hands were shaking, as she pulled out some bills and counted out two fives and a ten. She handed over the crumpled, dirty money, and said, "Who are they, Paco? Police, the military?"

"Don't ask," Paco said as he walked away. When he got back in the car, the men gestured for them to drive around the cement blockade. They all waved goodbye to Paco, and one yelled out, "*Saludos, amigo. Cuida a la gringa.*"

Elsa had shrugged off Paco's attempts to look out for her, other times it was harder to shake off the 'father figure' role he beamed. Now she was reminded that she couldn't make this journey without him. Even just a few years ago, when much of the country was marred with 'red zones', it would have been completely impossible to make the trip, even with Paco as her escort.

Elsa and Paco finally arrived at Salvatore's former hacienda, which was now a small town. They pulled over on the main street near the plaza, and immediately they drew attention. As they got out of the car, people began to trickle out of their homes and small businesses, and soon surrounded them in a relaxed yet interested manner, chatting with one another and gesturing toward the new arrivals.

Elsa stammered to find the appropriate explanation for her visit. She was unsure how the community would react to an offspring of the former *patrón*. She was relieved to find the villagers friendly, and they smiled and shook her hand as she declared Salvatore Santos her great-grandfather.

They stood in front of the medical clinic, a small building painted white with a bright red cross on the front. Their arrival lured the doctor outside. He wore a white medical jacket and black dress pants.

He introduced himself formally, "Good afternoon, my name is Dr. Gustavo Larco. If you need anything, please don't hesitate to ask." The doctor shook Elsa's hand and slightly bowed his head. She was surprised that he spoke perfect English.

Elsa couldn't help but notice his dark features and deep-set eyes. He was slender and tall, and she found him handsome. She felt herself blush.

"Thank you, that's very kind. My name is Elsa León. My great-grandfather founded the old hacienda, and I'm here to visit our family's country house, which used to be the main house. Maybe you could point me in the right direction?"

"I'm sorry, but I'm not familiar with the original layout of the estate. I wouldn't know the house off the top of my head," the doctor said.

"The Gomez Family lives there now, perhaps you know them?" Elsa persisted.

"Hernán and Meli Gomez?" the doctor asked with a grin. "Ah, yes. They live just outside of town, up the road a bit. They have a nice piece of property, good crops and an orchard, not to mention the silk production. Meli is known in these parts for her weaving. The women gather there, and she helps them sell their goods in a cooperative."

Elsa then saw a woman emerge from the clinic. She was petite and pretty, and wearing a bright floral nursing scrub top with jeans and sneakers. The young woman smiled at Elsa.

Gustavo said, "Olga, let me introduce you." Elsa and Olga greeted one another with a polite handshake. He continued, "Olga works in the clinic two days a week. She's a nurse practitioner and lives in Abancay."

"Abancay?" Elsa asked.

"Yes, it's the nearest city. About 50 miles north of here," Gustavo explained.

Elsa couldn't help but notice that Olga was attractive. She had large, almond shaped eyes and a pretty smile. Olga stood quietly for a moment, and then said to Gustavo, "I'm going to start heading home. I'll see you Thursday."

"Yes, of course, it's getting late. You don't want to miss the last *colectivo.*" Gustavo and Olga quickly pecked on the cheek, and she went back inside the clinic.

The doctor was smiling broadly now, and seemed more relaxed. He turned to Elsa and asked, "Before you head to the house, maybe you would like a tour of the town? It won't take long."

Elsa glanced around, looking for Paco. She spotted him resting on a bench across the way, his head resting on his chest. Besides, Elsa was intrigued with the town.

"Well, it looks as though Paco is taking a nap. A tour would be lovely."

"Great, let's stroll up the road this way toward the plaza."

"Would you like an Inca Kola?" a woman from the corner bodega called to her.

Before Elsa could answer the woman trotted over and handed her a bottle of the sweet fluorescent yellow soda that looked like toxic waste, but that had the distinct taste of cotton candy and banana. The pride Peruvians felt about their national soda pop was akin to the British with their tea. Some went so far as to claim the soda had medicinal properties, even though it looked radioactive.

Elsa took a sip and then grimaced.

The doctor laughed and said, "I know it's *awful stuff.* I'm sure you'd prefer tea."

"Where did you learn English?" Elsa asked.

"I studied and I did my residency in Boston. I was there for many years before deciding to move back to Peru."

"How did you end up here? I mean, I'm sorry, I don't mean to offend…" Elsa's voice trailed off as she realized that her question might seem condescending.

The doctor just smiled and chuckled once again. "I know it may seem like an odd choice, living in this tiny village in the middle of the Andes, but I felt like giving back to my country. There's so much poverty and need. The people here are practically forgotten about by the government. They receive very few resources, and what they do receive usually comes from foreign aid. It's absurd really."

Elsa nodded, but stayed quiet. She enjoyed his pleasing manner, but instinctively her guard was building. She didn't want to feel any attraction.

"You think I'm an idealist. But I needed some adventure in my life, and though most days are uneventful and slow, it's still exciting to me." He grinned at Elsa warmly.

Gustavo led her into the chapel, which was dark and gloomy with large straw crosses leaning against the walls, discarded leftovers of a religious procession. He showed Elsa the plaque covering Salvatore's remains. The plaque was chipped and scratched, and the adobe walls of the church seemed to resist crumbling down.

In the dimness, Elsa noticed an old lady sitting on a bench toward the front of the altar, facing a statue of the Virgin. It was so peaceful and calm, Elsa felt drawn to go and sit near her on the bench. They sat in silence, yet Elsa could hear the woman's faint prayers in Quechua. The woman was ancient with pure white hair, hunched over with rosary beads in her tiny crinkled hands.

Elsa was taken aback when, after a few moments, the woman scooted closer to Elsa and croaked in Spanish, "You belong to the Santos Family?"

"Yes, Salvatore was my great-grandfather." Elsa spoke loudly.

"You don't have to yell. I don't see so well, but my hearing is fine."

"Oh, of course, I'm sorry."

The lady laughed at that. "We haven't had anyone from the family visit since Lucía died, that would be some thirty years ago–except her sons, but they didn't stay long."

"You knew my great-grandmother?" Elsa turned to face the old woman.

"Of course, I did. All of us older folks knew her. She was the most generous person I've ever known, not to mention her lovely daughter Angelica. That girl was a true angel and one of my best friends. We were the same age." The woman smiled, and Elsa noticed the gaping hole where teeth once were.

"May I ask you about the plague that wiped out the hacienda? Was that during your time? It must have been a horrible thing." Elsa rubbed at her knees anxiously.

The woman slowly pulled herself up, still hunched over and began to shuffle away.

"I'm sorry if I said something to upset you," Elsa called out to her.

The woman stopped and turned around. She said, "The plague was not a Thing, it was a She."

The woman left Elsa sitting on the bench, pondering the strange declaration.

Just then Gustavo appeared, telling her, "Come outside, I have something to show you."

Back in the bright plaza, Elsa was intrigued by the street sign 'Calle Santos,' named after Salvatore Santos, and by the adjoining perpendicular street sign called 'Avenida Velasco'. Velasco was just one of the presidents who partitioned haciendas and gave land back to the Indians, which was how the town came to be. How befitting that both men squarely faced one another, each laying their claim to the town with stubborn tenacity.

As they continued their walking tour, Gustavo pointed out the community center, a large room where dances, raffles, and meetings were held. On a large blackboard in front of the building, written in chalk was the announcement: *Town Fair and raffle on Saturday: First Place–Young bull, three years old. Second Place–Old bull. Third Place–A goat. Fourth Place–A rooster. Fifth Place–A Surprise.* Elsa wondered what the *Surprise* might be.

Gustavo showed her buildings that at one time housed the Indians working on the hacienda, rather like slaves, she supposed. Elsa tried to remember something of the town, but her recollection was far too hazy. She must have walked these streets as a little girl, but she had no memory of it. Would someone there remember her as a child? It felt completely foreign to her. Then she tried to imagine the place as a thriving estate with Salvatore wearing a large sombrero, mounting an impressive stallion and yelling out orders. Her imagination contrived such pictures of him, although her image was developed more out of the cliché than any real truth.

While standing in front of the building, Elsa asked Gustavo, "Do you know anything about the Plague?"

"Oh that. It's a bit of local folklore."

"But it wasn't a disease. I just heard it was a person?"

"Well, the story the townsfolk tell is that Lucía had an aunt. She was a spinster that was sent by the family to supposedly help Lucía with her children as a nursemaid, but Esther turned out to have her own ambitions."

Then Gustavo began to tell the story about that night when the half moon disappeared on a cloudless night and a puma possessed the soul of a woman…

After the wedding of Lucía and Salvatore, Aunt Esther arrived at the hacienda with her niece. She spent the first weeks observing the goings on at the hacienda. Then on one otherwise peaceful day, a day when all of the colors sparkled under the sun, and the insects hummed contently as they carried out their enigmatic activities, suddenly a dark cloud washed over the brilliance of the sun and the insects abruptly ceased their reverberating song. Esther stormed into Salvatore's study.

"I believe the time has come, Salvatore. I have been standing by, observing the inner workings of this small industry-and I must say I am highly displeased," she began.

Salvatore stood up from his desk, prepared to let her fury wash over him. The nervous tic he had developed since she arrived made his right eye twitch.

"I have been silent up until now to the lazy, insubordinate attitude of these natives, who lack any work ethics. Look outside, and you will see at this very moment, the manner in which they all congregate in the square to gossip and pass around the pitchers of chicha. It is four o'clock in the afternoon, several hours of daylight left, and they stand around as if the day is done. I can't stand the lackadaisical approach with which you manage this estate any longer, and if you don't step in to discipline them, you can be sure that I will."

With that said, Esther stormed out of his study. She marched out the front door, and to Salvatore's complete shock and horror began an attack against the Indians with a long, leather horsewhip in hand. Right there in the plaza, she twirled herself about in a strange, demonic dance. In her long black satin dress with ruffles of lace and gray wisps of hair falling out of her bun, she seemed to be hissing and hurling thunderbolts at the Indians from her eyes. She lashed out with the horsewhip, and actually hit one woman in the leg. As the woman cried out, chaos ensued, with people running in all directions, screaming and carrying off their crying children.

Esther danced around the plaza, flogging anything that crossed her path.

After the incident, the Indians kept to themselves. They no longer congregated in the plaza to gossip or barter. Salvatore knew that they still convened, but it was no longer carefree and spontaneous. They met in the fields or along the dirt road, which led out of the valley and to the closest town, fifty-seven miles away.

He could hear their laughter and music discreetly floating out of the orange and lemon groves along the creek, hidden from view. At night, he saw the firelight and smoke billowing from their bonfires on the road where they danced and told jokes. It made Salvatore feel lonely and strangely envious of their fellowship, which he could never share with them. He missed their presence in the small square, the heart of the hacienda, which now stood dark and gloomy. It was like a ghost town, abandoned and eerily quiet.

There should be children playing, animals frolicking, and people of all ages greeting each other with friendly exchanges, he thought. But instead there was heaviness in the air, as if a cold, gray fog had descended upon the valley. This fog coalesced and unfolded itself over Acutambo like a weighty blanket.

Salvatore knew that a hacienda is like a village, and like any village it functioned in rhythm to its surroundings. Where there was nature, there was a distinct pulse in synchronicity with the warbling streams and creatures cavorting. The hum of nature set the beat to shovels and picks, and the pace of looms spinning, and brooms sweeping across bricks and stones.

There was a natural flow to the early morning activity which ever so slightly slowed and unwound until by midday all the world seemed to be functioning in one wave of easy, methodical motion. There was no resistance in this rhythm, just everything working together in a gentle hum. Esther was a thunderbolt in the midst of this delicate balance, disrupting the harmony of nature and causing a clamor wherever she went.

The Indians were the first to notice the changes and bad omens transforming the hacienda. The crops began to decline, and the water in the stream was drying up. The orange groves no longer produced in sweet, juicy abundance; the fruit was scarce, puny and bitter. The moths' procreation was similarly scarce and unfruitful.

After only a few weeks, Salvatore entered one of the adobe sheds where the silk worms were cared after. The room was arid and warm. Wooden plank beds filled the space and Salvatore slowly walked around them, peering at each bed lined with coarse paper and scattered with hundreds of gray moths.

The poor creatures now flapped their wings in desperation, as they each searched out a mate. The caretakers gently lifted or nudged the moths, trying to guide the males and females, so that they lay close enough for their instincts to guide to them. But they would not join. The specks of barren eggs lay scattered across the plank beds.

The moths' reproduction, even under normal conditions, was a tragic endeavor. As they emerged from their cocoons, metamorphosed from grotesque worms into unattractive, bland moths, there was a narrow window of opportunity for propagation. Normally, the females released their fertilized eggs, smaller than grains of rice, and then would abruptly die. The males expired long before. The entire process took only hours from emergence to death, and was all the more tragic when futile.

Salvatore swore under his breath, "It's a damn plague!"

It was as if a curse had been cast against the estate, and the Indians blamed it on Esther. The Plague rode on her muscular horse throughout the hacienda. She took to wearing trousers instead of dresses, long black boots and a big felt hat, and wielded the ominous, snake-like horsewhip. She rode with might and power, cursing at the Indians as they worked in the fields, transported bundles, or collected water from the vanishing stream. God forbid she found an idler or worse yet a drunk, for all the fury of hell would be unleashed upon them.

Chapter 5

Back at the car, Elsa said, "It was wonderful to meet you, Gustavo. I hope to see you again. Once I'm settled, maybe you and your wife could join me for dinner."

"That would be very nice, though I'm not married. It's just me, I'm afraid. But I do look forward to meeting your husband. Will he be joining you here in Peru?" Gustavo said as he looked down toward Elsa's hand.

She was vacantly twirling her wedding band, a habit she had developed. Elsa jerked her hand away from the ring, and chirped nervously, "Oh, maybe. He has a lot of work at the moment. I really don't know." Elsa felt her face flush with heat, and she knew she was glowing red with embarrassment. Elsa knew she was hiding behind the ring. She wasn't ready for romance, and she felt a strong attraction to the doctor.

Gustavo just smiled, with the same easy manner as before. "In any case, dinner would be wonderful."

"Maybe you'd like to come with Olga?" Elsa asked, unsure of their relationship.

"That would be difficult. She has to catch the bus to Abancay before five o'clock. Her family expects her home."

"Sounds like it'll be just the two of us, in that case. I'll see you again soon." Elsa worried that she sounded girlish.

"I look forward to it," and with that said, he leaned in for a kiss on the cheek. Of course, this was as customary as a handshake, but this time Elsa felt awkward, and suddenly shy.

She watched the kind doctor enter the clinic, and she felt a strange pang. She wondered about his relationship with Olga. Did the reference to her family mean that she had a husband and children? Most young people in Peru stay living at home if they're single, so the reference could have easily meant her parents. But anyway, it didn't really matter since Elsa wasn't ready to let her armor down, especially with a Latin man. Though she hated to stereotype, they were known to be womanizers. If Charles couldn't stay faithful, she would never trust a Latino to do any better. She was callous as she told herself that Gustavo probably had a girlfriend, even a wife tucked away somewhere. It was a good thing she had worn the ring.

She and Paco were once again on their way. The country house was only a couple of miles away. Elsa took out her journal from the bag on the backseat of Paco's taxi, and opened it to the page with Aunt Lina's small, fine script. Aunt Lina's directions to the house were hardly legible, and Paco seemed better able to decipher the hand-drawn map.

He tried to read the map while driving as a truck approached on the other side of the two-lane road. Elsa glanced up just in time to see their car swerve slightly into the other lane.

"*Paco, cuidado.*" Elsa grabbed the steering wheel, giving it a gentle pull toward her.

"*Por Dios.* These truckers have no courtesy, and they should slow down." Paco didn't seem to realize that he was the one who had drifted into the other lane and that the truck had been driving at a snail's pace.

Elsa shuddered from the near head-on collision.

It had taken Elsa days to reach the house. The Acutambo Hacienda of a bygone era was now a wistful, tarrying town. In some ways Elsa thought she had been delaying, drawing out her encounter with her great-grandmother's country house so as to savor it more. It was like meeting with an old lover: the apprehension and the excitement keeps one dawdling in front of the mirror, or searching and fumbling for something intangible just to extend the anticipation. Then there would be the sweet encounter, exhilarating and also sentimental.

Now they were only a few minutes away and Elsa built up the moment, imagining the place to her liking and everything that would follow.

They were surrounded by green rolling hills, adobe houses and crops. There were pastures with cows and fields of sunflowers in spectacular bloom. Then as they continued, passing horses and a sow with her piglets on the side of the road, there it was. Paco pulled up slowly. Aunt Lina had sent the family word of Elsa's visit, so they were expecting her.

The house was just as she remembered it. It was made of adobe bricks with a red-clay tiled roof. There was a second story with a long balcony protruding out, ornately carved from a rich wood. Bougainvillea in deep purple grew in abundance and draped over the entire side of the house, and the covered porch stood invitingly with the door wide open. Paco tooted the car horn. A few minutes later, the Gomez family came outside and stood on the porch. The family waited, standing slightly stiff and formal to greet Elsa.

The caretakers had lived there for many years, and Elsa thought her arrival might seem not only odd but also intrusive. How would the family feel to have a member of the Santos family show up, and especially as an heir to the small estate?

"*Bienvenida, Señora,*" they said, welcoming Elsa into the home.

Hernán Gomez walked with a slight limp; he was close to sixty years old. He immediately started helping Paco unload

Elsa's luggage, and then carried her bags through the front door. Elsa stood admiring his three small children and his much younger wife, Meli.

Paco hollered to Elsa as he strolled back to his car, "Elsita, I'm going to go back into town to pick up a few things from the *bodega.* Anyway, It will give you some time to get acquainted with things. You'll be okay, I think."

"Yes, I'll be fine here." Elsa reassured him. She felt nervous yet also comfortable enough. Even though the family was reserved, they were pleasant. She would get to know them and the house while he was gone.

Paco waved as he drove off.

Elsa walked through the house, taking in the memories there. She held her breath slightly as Meli led her to the staircase and to the upstairs bedrooms, where she had had so many impressions as a little girl. She could almost feel Angelica's kiss on her forehead as her grandmother tucked her into bed, almost hear the tap of Lucía's cane against the wood floor.

There were three bedrooms upstairs. The first was a large open room with hardwood floors and white stucco walls, with a balcony with a magnificent view of the expansive fields, like a quilt stretched out before her. Elsa admired the snow-capped mountains in the distance. She paused a moment to let the sunshine warm her face.

Elsa knew this was the room she'd choose to use while she was there. It was airy and filled with light.

Meli explained, "This is the main bedroom, but now I'll show you Lucía's room."

"You mean that Lucía didn't use the master bedroom?" Elsa asked as they walked to the room across the short hallway. That room was charming, but much smaller, with only one window facing the main road. Elsa persisted, "This was Lucía's room? Why didn't she use the master bedroom, Meli?"

Elsa then remembered her great-grandmother's tiny bedroom with its twin-size bed. She could sense once again, in her mind's eye, Lucía walking with her cane, the sound of the thump and tap against the hardwood floor, and Pastor, the old crippled German Shepard, following behind her.

Meli stayed quiet, looking at Elsa with a serious expression, contemplating her response. Elsa poked around the room, opening the drawers of the small dresser, and looking under the bed.

Finally Meli answered, "Lucía said that the other room is visited by spirits. She had become frightened."

The ghosts? Elsa felt a wave of fear rush through her body. In some ways, she felt ridiculous harboring such beliefs, but the family was convinced and frightened by the history of the house and so she couldn't help herself. She wondered in which room the murder had taken place, as she peered around each corner and they made their way down the creaking staircase.

Soon they were passing through the kitchen. They walked out the door of the kitchen to the back of the house, as Hernán explained the property grounds. Memories of the place continued to flood back. The courtyard, where she had sat with Lucía, was still strewn with ropes where laundry hung to dry, and the passion fruit vines twisted upward toward the roof, laden and heavy with fruit. Elsa remembered holding a basket, while her great-uncle José stood on a short ladder and picked the ripe fruit, filling the basket until Elsa's arms ached. Then Angelica made a pitcher of passion fruit juice, which Elsa gulped down.

Elsa now noticed how well kept and tidy the place was, even with the chicken coop and two goats. There was a mutt walking alongside her, and she was reminded of Pastor, who would surely be buried in the backyard somewhere. The mutt tired of the excitement and trotted back into the house. The barefoot children followed Elsa, silent and serious, one trailing a long piece of rope behind her.

Meli kept her head tilted down and her eyes averted. Yet once their eyes met, Elsa was taken aback by her dark penetrating depth. Elsa felt drawn into Meli's gaze, until Meli pulled away.

Elsa then realized that Meli and Hernán were guarded, and they never smiled at her. They both wore stern expressions. Most likely, they felt threatened by her visit.

Elsa couldn't reassure them, and tell them that she had no intention of kicking them out of the only home their children had known. Selling the house seemed like the best option, but what would happen to the family? She wondered where they would live. But then Elsa told herself that the family wasn't really her responsibility. Surely they would find their way. People move all the time. Things change; that's the nature of life. Elsa knew that better than anyone. And just maybe, once the house sold, the new owners would keep the family as hired help.

Elsa still watched Meli, noticing her hands. A golden iridescence, like a fine powder, speckled her fingertips.

Hernán explained his duties around the property, and Elsa enjoyed the quiet demeanor and slow beat of his hypnotic voice as they strolled through the yard. He pointed out the corn crop in the near distance.

Elsa finally interrupted him. "As you may already know, my brother and I have inherited the house from my grandmother. But we still don't have any plans for the property. For now, your family can continue to live here, and take care of the place just as you have been. I'll notify you as soon as possible, once we've decided what we're going to do. Is that okay with you?" Elsa wanted to clear the air. She wished she could give them more reassurance, but it was the best she could do for now. At least she wasn't hiding anything.

Elsa saw the look of hesitation in the couple's eyes, as they nodded at each other and then at her in agreement. She was glad to clarify things and get that off her chest. And she hoped they'd warm up to her soon.

"I plan to stay for a few weeks, about a month," she added.

Hernán said, "I'll continue to tend to the grounds and the animals, and Meli will cook and clean the house. Does that suit you, *señora?*"

"Yes, very much. But please call me Elsa."

"*Está bien, señora. Gracias,*" Hernán answered back.

Hernán pointed out the small house where they lived, just off the main house, and which sat right next to the nearly mythical shed of her childhood memories. Their house was simple, but also charming, with its own small porch and garden patch.

Elsa was breathless as she opened the door of the silkworm shed and peeked inside. She saw the wooden beds housing silkworms. She approached the flatbeds, and in the dim light could see that one was filled with tiny specks of silkworm eggs strewn over newspaper. Another bed was scattered with branches, and large white worms were busy at work weaving their cocoons. Another contained moths, males and females, flapping around, some joined together, others still searching for a mate. Elsa shuddered at the sight of the moths, so desperate to cling together.

Elsa and Hernán stood side by side motionless in the quiet room watching the moths, with faint light from the doorway glowing off translucent wings. Suddenly Elsa felt a strange sensation at the base of her neck. She felt something crawling through her hair, tugging ever so slightly and grazing her skin. She froze and with a slight whimper, said, "Excuse me, Hernán, but I think there's something on me." She couldn't breathe.

Hernán leaned toward her, and very casually poked through her long hair. Quickly he pinched a large bug off her and flicked it across the room, telling her, "That's a scorpion. There are a lot around here, so be careful, they're poisonous." He walked out of the room, leaving Elsa alone. She tried to catch her breath.

Slowly she walked to the dark corner where the scorpion had landed, and she began to examine the dirt floor. She wanted to see it, but then wondered to herself why. It had crawled through her hair, brushed her neck with its long body, but it didn't bite her. It was better not to get its image stuck in her mind.

Outside, mulberry trees grew tall, shading the shed with lush leafy branches. Elsa strolled through the backyard filled with fruit trees: avocado, papaya, and lime. There were bushes of blackberries and hearty vines of passion fruit. She admired the small but healthy crop of corn. Gradually she began to shake off the fear of the scorpion. She worked to regain her composure.

The property was in good condition, so she considered what the market value of the place would be if she sold it. Selling the house seemed like a good option. Elsa knew her brother would jump at the chance, and maybe it made the most sense. Elsa felt an attachment to the place, to all of the memories there, but how could she ever manage to keep it? She lived so far away.

It was approaching dusk as she strolled through the back-yard, admiring the foliage and green life surrounding her. The reclining sun was casting a golden glow, as if everything was brimming with honey, drenched and dripping in a sunlit bath overflowing with the rich, flowery syrup from a radiant source. All of nature and the vast pink sky were set aglow, and even the long shadows seemed lit-up from the inside turning empty darkness into luminous, vibrant life.

Elsa took Meli's smallest child by the hand, and the little doll-like toddler grasped her fingers as they stood in the shimmering and tall, green stalks of corn. Elsa took in a deep breath of the sweet moistness and the baby mimicked her as she closed her eyes and exhaled slowly.

Meli appeared and lifted up the toddler, saying, " Leave the *señora* alone– don't bother her." She began to walk away, carrying off the child.

"It's okay, I don't mind. And call me Elsa," she called out. But Meli had already disappeared.

That same evening, Elsa settled in and sent Paco on his way. He left reluctantly, worried about leaving her in that remote place. She reminded him that she wasn't alone.

Paco gave her a firm hug and patted the top of her head in a parental gesture, and then he climbed into the dusty old car. He was soon rambling off in the beat-up automobile, spewing smoke and a loud rattle from the muffler. He bounced down the road as Hernán, Meli, the children, and Elsa stood waving goodbye until he disappeared out of sight.

Elsa kneeled at the children. "I'll be staying here for a little while, is that all right with you?" she asked them with a smile.

The three nodded shyly and the eldest, Ruth, took Elsa's hand, opened her palm and traced her lifeline with a tiny finger. This startled Elsa, then they all began to laugh. Elsa noticed Meli shaking her head and looking at them with dis-approval.

Within the first couple of days, Elsa had to adjust to certain inconveniences. The bathroom had modern day fixtures, though they were old and rusty, but the first time she showered, she was confronted with an unexpected problem. There was only one shower handle, and she asked Meli, "Where is the hot water handle?"

Meli looked at Elsa confused. "Hot water?"

"There's hot water, isn't there?" Elsa hadn't imagined the other possibility. In Lima, and even along the tourist route in the Andes, bathrooms were equipped with water heaters, so although there was a process of turning on the thermos and sometimes waiting up to twenty minutes for hot water, it was generally available. Elsa then realized there was no thermos switch, no heater in sight.

Mountain water is cold, so Elsa quickly learned to sit in the sunshine on the porch to dry her hair. No luxurious hot showers, just quick, icy waters to start the day.

Another morning, Elsa turned the knob of the sink and no water came out. The pipes inside the wall groaned. She tried again, and nothing. Elsa made her way into the kitchen, and turned the sink handle. No water.

"Meli, *lo siento mucho,* but I need help," she called out the back porch, where she saw Meli a short distance away taking laundry down from the cord.

"*Si, Doña Elsa, que pasa?*"

"The water won't turn on," Elsa explained.

"Of course not, they're rationing today. There won't be water until tomorrow morning."

Elsa was surprised by Meli's casual explanation.

"Nobody told me. Rationing? Is this something they do often?"

"Yes, often. Sometimes the water level gets too low."

It was early July, and the middle of the dry season, so rationing would be often. It wouldn't be until December, when the rainy season began with the summer months, that creeks and rivers would swell, and mudslides would become a concern.

"Is there a rationing schedule?"

"No schedule." Meli folded the towel in her hand.

"Do they tell you in advance?" Elsa didn't even know who 'they' were, but figured the town had to have some means of announcing, by television or radio.

"Sometimes they tell us by radio, but not always. Our neighbor usually loses water first, her house sits on the hill so she hollers to let me know." Meli wandered over to the side of her small house, and came back carrying a large bucket filled with water.

"Here you go, Doña Elsa. You can use this," Meli said, as she placed the bucket inside the porch door. "Remember, you'll have to use this water to flush the toilet."

Elsa thanked Meli, and then groaned. She went back to her room, and sat at the foot of the bed. She was tempted to climb back into the bed, cover her head and sleep the rest of the day.

She just didn't have it in her, so many inconveniences and hardships, without simple amenities. Was she really so soft, so incapable? It had only been a few days since her arrival, and Elsa was glad she was only visiting. Even though a simpler life was appealing in many ways, she already missed the ease of life back in the States.

That very same night, while Elsa lay awake staring at the ceiling, she tried to calm the thoughts running through her mind. She began to feel the pull of sleep, as she rolled over. But when she turned over, she saw a distinct dark shadow move across the white stucco wall. The black figure was thin and tall, and appeared to be looking down at her as it slowly glided from the foot of the bed toward her. Elsa let out a meek cry and shut her eyes. She rolled over again and tucked her knees into her belly. As she lay there, trying to catch her breath, she began to hear a quiet weeping coming from across the room. She willed herself to open her eyes, and there at the foot of the bed she saw a faint figure kneeling with his hands in prayer. Elsa didn't feel as frightened by this strange hazy image, as she did by the shadow. The whispering prayers actually lulled her to sleep.

As the days passed, Elsa began to think of her visitors as restless dreams. Most nights she heard the gentle weeping, and sometimes saw the faint figure kneeling at the foot of her bed. Yet the tall, black shadow terrified her, and on those nights that the apparition appeared, Elsa felt unnerved and exhausted the next day.

Elsa beat herself down for not being stronger. She willed herself to face each day with determination and strength. She envied Meli, as she watched her take care of the house and her family with such calm and proficiency.

Meli hadn't warmed up to Elsa. Elsa could only imagine the things running through Meli's mind: spoiled *gringa*, soft American. Maybe she just doesn't like me, Elsa thought. Or maybe it's just her nature to be reserved. Elsa felt lonely, especially when she heard the family laughing and playing out back while she was alone inside the house. Elsa wished it could be different.

Elsa fought doubts about her future—about making decisions with the house, about the Gomez's coldness toward her, and those strange dreams—by spending her days in the garden. It reminded her of her own vegetable patch at her cabin in northern California, where she grew tomatoes, herbs, and various types of lettuces and squashes.

One early morning, Elsa inspected the plots, picking ripe avocados and papayas from the trees, checking plants for insects, watering the soil, removing weeds and dry debris. She wore a large straw hat, sturdy canvas gloves, and muddy sandals. She toiled for hours surrounded by garden scents. She paused weeding, and watched the mule and plow guided by Hernán a short distance away. The old mule stumbled across the thirsty dirt pulling up hearty weeds from the field. Elsa thought, let me help you, beast of burden. Let me walk alongside as you selflessly work my land. Then Elsa decided that she was not bold enough to call it her own land, and so she continued to watch from a distance.

Elsa then accompanied Hernán as he tended to the silkworms. He worked in silence, making sure there were plenty of mulberry leaves to satiate their voracious hunger. It reminded her of watching her great-uncle José as he placed the fresh, green leaves in the plank beds, and then later small branches where the worms would weave their cocoons. Now Elsa noticed that the worms were growing ever larger and stronger. They looked pale, yet with a slight golden iridescence, and like chubby fingers waving at her.

That evening, Elsa looked out over the balcony, overlooking the backyard trees and crops. It was one of her favorite spots. And the master bedroom had natural light and an airiness that Elsa found refreshing. She could hear the children laughing and squealing somewhere below. Elsa sat there until it turned dark, and then went to her bed to read.

Like so many other nights, Elsa got that strange feeling. She looked up from her book to see the dark, tall shadow move slowly across the wall, with its angular head seeming to look down at her. She shuddered. Elsa pulled the blanket up over her and rolled onto her side. She closed her eyes tightly and willed herself to breathe deeply.

In the silence, Elsa could hear feet pacing the room and that familiar gentle sobbing. She slowly pulled the blanket down and peered over her shoulder. She knew she'd see him. There was the same silhouette of a figure kneeling at the foot of her bed. She sat up with a start.

Then something caught her eye at the doorway, which was opened a crack. A short, dark figure moved away. Elsa thought it was Meli, but what would she be doing standing outside the door of her bedroom? Elsa once again attributed all of this to her imagination and the effects of spending too much time alone. She shook off her fears and insecurities.

The next morning, as she lay in bed staring at the ceiling, Elsa caught herself twirling her wedding band absentmindedly. She suddenly felt angry. She was annoyed that in a slight way she was still relying on Charles, and she had grown tired of its constant reminder. She pulled the ring off, noticing that her tan left a white indentation in its place. She put the ring back in her jewelry bag. It had served its purpose. However, she knew that she would wear it again when she traveled back home.

Chapter 6

In the village surrounding the house, Elsa came to find solace in the locals who strolled along the dirt roads, and among her neighbors who lived in the adobe houses whitewashed and painted with political propaganda. Slogans and acronyms of political parties–communist, right wing, or somewhere in between–were all written out in bold red, black and white. Chickens and cows ran loose, as did children. Here they all referred to her as *Mamá* Elsa, a title of respect exalting her to the position of matriarch.

Elsa fit into that world where nature was dominant and the Indians were reclusive. I'm not one of them, she thought, and being different, they tended to keep her at a polite distance. Do I miss California? Elsa asked herself. Her cabin in the woods in the small town of Eureka seemed much lonelier, and a sequestered place compared to the Andes.

The nature in Peru was formidable, yet it stood intimately in the company of humans and beasts, which made it friendlier and more hospitable than the thick, dark woods. Now the redwood forests seemed almost cryptic and foreboding in comparison to the mountains, so fresh and open to life.

Whereas the lush forests were a world of decay and mysterious regeneration of ancient life, seemingly prehistoric with fungi, spores, ferns and towering trees hundreds of years old, the Andes were young in comparison: with flowers blooming, crops producing, herds of wild vicuñas roving a magnificent expanse. Elsa suspected she might suffocate in a cloistered blanket of forest, and claustrophobia would overtake her after adapting to this open terrain with its eternal crisp air and clear celestial skies.

The first time the women arrived to the house to weave, Elsa watched them with wonder from a discreet corner of the patio. They arrived wearing colorful garments and carrying an assortment of bundles and baskets, and seated themselves in a circle on the patio, hardly glancing at Elsa. Some sat on the floor cross-legged, while the elders sat on stools and chairs. Meli brought out two looms from her room, so that while some spun the thread, others wove. Some of the women knitted yarn with small metal needles, which clinked together in quiet synchronicity.

Elsa learned that the glow on Meli's fingertips came from the weaving of the silk at the loom. Elsa watched as the women worked to make the most wondrous golden-hued ponchos, scarves, and variety of *prendas*.

Elsa had a vision of Lucía, sitting in her rocking chair, spinning the bundles into fine thread. Now it was a handful of local women who spun and wove, and knitted golden, fine garments to be sold at the marketplace.

Elsa sat with them, placing herself just outside their close circle. She didn't want to intrude, and the women hardly seemed to notice her. Yet, when the women gathered their materials together, and then rose to their feet to leave, a small line of older ladies went to Elsa. They took turns shaking her hands warmly, some giving her slight hugs, as they introduced them-selves. Many of these women told Elsa that they remembered her as a little girl. One elder, after giving Elsa a gentle hug, said, "Doña Elsa, I knew your great-grandmother well. She was my son's godmother. I used to hold you and play with you. Do you remember me?"

Elsa examined the woman, noticing the faint lines on her face, her white teeth and long black hair, without a single strand of gray. Many of the elders hardly aged, usually one noticed the years in their hands. The woman's hands were ancient.

Elsa smiled warmly and said, "I'm sorry, it was so long ago. I was very young."

"Yes, that's true." The woman gave her a pat on the arm.

Meli gathered the silk bundles, still with her fingertips glowing with fine, golden powder. Soon the patio was empty, and Elsa helped Meli place the looms back in her house.

When the women left, Meli began her housework. This always made Elsa feel uncomfortable, and so Elsa insisted on helping her. Meli resisted help; it was unheard of for a matron to do chores alongside the maid.

"*Ay, Doña Elsa, dejeme hacerlo*. Let me sweep, *por favor*," Meli whined as she took the broom from Elsa. She was truly baffled by Elsa's insistence, and also seemed annoyed.

"I'd like to do it myself." Elsa took the broom back. This little struggle went on for a few moments until finally Meli gave in.

Elsa opened one of the cabinets in the kitchen, looking for a plastic bag for garbage. She screamed and suddenly jumped back, nearly falling on her rear. Her heart was racing, as she watched a huge black tarantula crawl out of the cabinet and move its way slowly across the kitchen floor. "Meli, help," was all Elsa could manage to squeak out, as several baby tarantulas followed behind the mother spider. Elsa couldn't move.

Without a moment's hesitation, Meli took the dustpan and scooped up all of the spiders together, the mother and its fat babies, and dumped them in the yard out back. When she came back in and checked inside the cabinet for any baby stragglers, she said, "Don't worry, tarantulas are not poisonous, just watch out for scorpions."

Elsa remembered then the sensation of the scorpion crawling inside her hair, grazing her skin, and she shuddered. Elsa had to admit that as frightened and surprised as she was by the tarantula, it was not nearly as scary as the scorpion. The tarantulas, in their own strange way, were beautiful creatures.

The next day, Meli saw Elsa in the kitchen preparing a salad for lunch. She got huffy and shook her head. "*Señora*, you are as stubborn as a tired mule."

Meli eventually resigned herself to Elsa's unusual habits of sweeping, dusting, preparing lunch, and helping her as she washed clothes in large buckets and hung them out in the sun to dry. She couldn't understand that it seemed just as unusual for Elsa to be waited on by another person.

Elsa watched Meli as she ironed clothes, admiring the single silky-smooth black braid that reached her waist. She was short and stocky but moved gracefully. Her complexion was delicious bronze with rosy cheeks, as if rouge was painted onto her skin. Her dark eyes sparkled.

"Let me iron," Elsa said to her.

"No, you are a terrible ironer." It was true. There were a lot of things Elsa discovered she didn't do well, compared to Meli's efficiency in all things domestic. She wasn't good at wringing out wet clothes (it made her shoulders ache) or making jam (it always boiled over and burned) or cutting up a whole chicken (it had to be de-feathered first!). Elsa didn't want a maid, but she needed Meli. Running a household in the Andes was a lot more work than at home. There was no washer or dryer or su-permarket with meats packaged neatly in plastic. Meli walked to the market every morning. Still, if they wanted chicken for lunch, Meli went to the coop and picked one out, wrung its neck, chopped off its head and drained the blood, then poured hot water over it to remove the feathers. She did it so fast that Elsa hardly even noticed, until it was already boiling in a pot redolent with herbs.

The children liked to collect the eggs from the coop. Hernán milked the goats. No one in the house drank goat milk, but they traded the milk with a neighbor for guinea pigs—which Elsa didn't eat. She liked to watch the children chase the guinea pigs around, though, as they all made a merry gurgling sound.

When she wasn't busy with the house, Meli quietly worked on the large frame, inviting Elsa to watch and learn as the silk threads interlaced into glowing fabric, a strange intimate dance of the warp and weft. Meli was a patient teacher. The time spent between them softened Meli, and she began to smile and laugh with Elsa, teasing her apprentice when Elsa became frustrated. Elsa felt awkward at first, as her threads tangled and she maneuvered the weft painstakingly slow, but gradually with practice her fingers became more dexterous and flexible as she learned the techniques of shedding, picking and battening on the vertical loom.

Elsa hadn't forgotten about the doctor and her promise to have dinner with him. She had tried to push Gustavo out of her mind, but she was feeling lonely. Not for romance necessarily, but for someone to talk with and share. Though she called Margot from her cell phone once in a while, her friend's voice still felt far away. It wasn't the same as real face-to-face with someone who shared in the same experiences. She felt nervous about her attraction to him, but then she reminded herself that he still thought she was married. She could use that as a safe buffer between them.

She called the clinic. Gustavo answered warmly and agreed to come to dinner the following evening.

The next day, Elsa and Meli worked together to prepare dinner for the doctor, who would be arriving soon. Elsa was jittery as she chopped onions and tomatoes for the pasta dish. Her stomach was in a tight knot, as she thought about the attraction she had felt for Gustavo.

Just as she was drifting into a daydream about the evening, Meli entered the kitchen holding a dead chicken by the neck.

"The black feathered hens make for the best tasting broth. I like to save them for special occasions," Meli told her. Whether it was true or just an old wives' tale, Elsa had no idea.

Hernán moved the dining room table out to the back porch, and Meli placed a vase of wildflowers and a candle on the table. The courtyard was cleared of clutter. Elsa began to realize their intentions. She asked them, "You'll be joining us for dinner, won't you?"

Hernán cleared his throat and muttered, "*Gracias–*" just as Meli kicked him in the ankle. He continued, "We won't be able to Doña Elsa. We will take the children to the plaza tonight for a dance." Elsa didn't argue, but that flutter in her gut intensified.

Gustavo arrived, wearing a white dress shirt and blue jeans with boots. Elsa greeted him warmly. She herself had dressed up a little, while trying to look like she wasn't trying too hard. She wore a skirt and silky blouse, with her long curls let loose down her back.

"I was relieved to finally get this invitation. I was afraid you had forgotten about me and would leave Peru without saying goodbye," Gustavo said playfully.

"I didn't forget," Elsa said coyly. She led him out to the courtyard, where the light of the candle cast a soft glow. "I didn't realize that the time would pass so quickly. I've been so busy adjusting to how things work here."

"Yes, I'm sorry I wasn't of any help. I guess your husband couldn't make the trip after all. But it looks like the Gomez Family has taken good care of you."

They were seated now at the table, and Elsa changed the subject by offering him a drink. "Would you like a glass of wine? Maybe beer? I wasn't sure what you'd drink, so I got both."

"Wine would be fantastic. It's not so easy to come by here. You must have good connections." Gustavo smiled, and Elsa reminded herself, *he thinks I have a husband.* She began to feel more at ease. She let go of her expectations and nerves, and began to enjoy herself.

"It's taken some time, but I'm learning the ropes. You'd be surprised what I can get my hands on. If you have any requests, just let me know." Elsa poured the wine into small water glasses. "I haven't found any wine glasses yet, though."

"This will do just fine."

"Cheers then. What shall we toast to?" Elsa held up her glass.

"To new friendships," Gustavo said.

"Yes, to friendship." Elsa clinked her glass with Gustavo's and they took a sip, while looking into each other's eyes–until Elsa self-consciously pulled her gaze away.

In no time, the two were spent from laughing, telling stories about their childhoods, about their lives in the States. Gustavo shared his experiences living in Boston, while Elsa told him about teaching in Northern California.

Gustavo said, "Your husband is missing out on all this. It's too bad for him." He poured more wine into Elsa's glass, and then into his own.

Elsa felt stuck. She really didn't feel like talking about the divorce; she knew it would change her mood. She stayed quiet a moment, taking a sip from her glass. Then she said, "Well, yes, he often does miss out. But I'm glad you're here." She smiled at Gustavo, and then rose to clear the table.

"I'm glad too," he replied. Gustavo helped her take the dishes to the kitchen.

Olga, Gustavo's partner at the clinic, also entered Elsa's mind. She still wondered about their relationship, but she felt too shy to ask him about it—and it might seem forward.

A few minutes later, they stood together on the front porch, looking up at the glittering nighttime sky.

Elsa told him, "One thing I still can't get used to is the magnificence of the night sky here. The southern hemisphere is so dense with stars; it's milky and brighter than the north. It takes my breath away every night."

"The beauty here takes my breath away, too," Gustavo said in a hushed voice.

Elsa looked over at him, and instead of gazing up at the sky, he was looking at her.

Elsa felt conflicted. She wanted to let her guard down, wanted the warmth and comfort of his presence to soothe her. Suddenly she felt him retreat from her, as he backed away.

"I must be going now," he announced firmly. He leaned forward and kissed her cheek quickly. "Thank you for a wonderful evening," he called out as he strode down the lane to his jeep. Elsa just stood and watched him go; she didn't know how to stop him.

Lucía and Salvatore started a family. The birth of their first son, José, nearly killed Lucía, and it took her several months to recover. So Salvatore was a nervous wreck with her second pregnancy. He feared this would be the one to take her life.

Lucía became weaker and frail as her stomach began to swell, until gradually her entire being was engulfed. Lucía shrank beneath the round mass. Esther kept her mostly in seclusion; only in the afternoons, when the weather was particularly mild, Lucía would appear lounging on the porch, in a daze and sipping one of the medicine woman Pancha's herbal concoctions.

One warm afternoon, lethargic flies swirled in huge circles, unable to narrow in on the pitcher of lemonade resting on the table. Lucía dozed on the chaise with a book spread over her chest, her huge belly obscuring her figure. Salvatore tiptoed so as not to wake her, and stood over his wife to admire her beautiful face.

"*Mi amor*," he whispered. Lucía stirred. "*Por favor*, stay strong for this child." Salvatore let the tears flow freely down his face. Lucía opened her eyes and she smiled at him. Salvatore was just about to kneel and place his hands over the bulge and plead to the life within to be merciful on his beloved, when the Plague marched up the steps.

"Salvatore, did you see Pedro today? It seems that he's been trying to catch a loose boar, and they're both tearing up the bean field. Are you going to handle this, or shall I?" While she spoke, Esther brusquely propped up Lucía and refilled her glass with the lemonade spiked with a dark green herb, which Pancha said would help induce labor.

Salvatore sighed. He had to handle it, because if he didn't Esther would find an excuse to shoot Pedro in the leg, or worse. He gave a quick glance to Lucía before leaving, and she appeared flushed and glassy eyed.

That night Lucía went into labor and the entire hacienda began a vigil. Everyone prepared for the long and torturous hours that lay ahead. Candles were lit in every house, and the women congregated in the chapel to pray before the Virgin for her compassionate intervention.

Salvatore had been ordered out of the bedroom, and so he stayed inside his study, muttering like a madman, pacing the room while dripping sweat and wringing his hands. But to Salvatore's astonishment, less than an hour had passed when there was a knock on the door.

The midwife called to him, "Don Salvatore, good news! You have a healthy baby daughter."

He ran from the study and into the bedroom. Pancha had gathered up her belongings, and the old woman was hunched over as she limped past him without looking up, making a clucking sound with her toothless mouth. She muttered, "All that fuss over nothing," and left the room.

Salvatore found Lucía in perfect spirits. She was glowing, smiling and even seemed to have gained a few pounds on her frame. She had never looked as strong and healthy. As she nursed the baby, she said, "I'm starved! I think I could chase down that pig and eat it myself."

And thus was the auspicious birth of their daughter, Angelica. Angelica seemingly was born a cherub, not a mortal child. Her bright eyes and rosy cheeks, and plump and perfect aspect of a baby girl delighted everyone. Salvatore was known to march her through the hacienda on his shoulders, just to show her off to the world.

There was a subtle transformation in the Plague with the arrival of a baby girl, such a light and comely influence over the saddened estate. One couldn't help but notice the contented way in which Esther whisked up Angelica, carrying out household chores while humming cheerfully under her breath.

Angelica was raised under the watchful eye of Esther, sheltered and over-protected. In her early years, she was forbidden to mingle with the Indian children and so Angelica spent most of her days alone within the big house. Rarely did her older brother or children from neighboring haciendas play with her. As she got older, she was known to run into the hillsides, looking for make-believe companions.

One day, Angelica roamed down to the creek, talking to herself in an animated and free-spirited way. She came to a small rock cave and stood at the entrance, just as her brother, José, came looking for her.

"What are you doing, Angelica? You shouldn't be down here all alone." He had walked down the trail, tracking Angelica's footprints in the dirt. The brush was damp and the roar of the creek could be heard, hidden behind the bushes.

"Did you see that little man in the cave? He was calling me, telling me to follow him," Angelica told her brother.

"What did he look like?" José asked, amused by his sister's imagination. Even so, he approached the small cave with apprehension. He stuck his head in and yelled, "Hello?"

"He was tiny with big ears and was dressed in a suit," Angelica explained wide-eyed.

José grabbed her by the hand and led her down the path as quickly as her little legs could carry her.

Then the story was passed down about the time a *duende* tried to kidnap Angelica. Lucía explained, "*Duendes* especially like bright, beautiful children. Angelica could have disappeared forever. You know, many children go missing. Who knows how many are taken by mischievous elves!"

Angelica wasn't frightened of the woods, yet she learned to keep a watchful eye. She believed in fairies and desperately wanted to encounter one. Whenever she had the good fortune of trapping a drifting seed from a dandelion clock, floating bright white like a feathery, tiny parachute or an iridescent big-eyed bug in the palm of her hand, they became magical creatures. Not as impressive as an elf, but not as menacing either.

Elsa called Margot from her cell phone, and their chat was escalating into a small argument. "It's almost August, and you still don't have a return date or ticket?" Margot pressed Elsa for a decision.

"I know, I know, but I still have time. Classes don't start for a few more weeks. And anyway, if there's low enrollment they might even be cancelled." Elsa reasoned.

"Yes, but you don't know that, Elsa. You have responsibilities. I mean, who am I to say, but it just seems odd that you've dropped off the map. Aren't you anxious to get back to your life?" Margot asked.

"Not really, Margot."

Elsa realized that she wasn't anxious at all to get back to life there. She missed Margot and some of her friends, but nothing was calling her back, and she felt happier than she had in a long time. The only worries hanging over her were those strange nightly visits, which she was gradually getting accustomed to, and Meli's odd appearance at her doorway during those fitful nights. Elsa pushed away fears, telling herself it was just her imagination.

"I don't want you to worry about me." Elsa lightened her tone. "Hey, did I tell you that I met a handsome single doctor?"

"You're kidding, right?"

Elsa was standing on her balcony, looking below at Hernán and the mule working in the fields. The mountain peaks loomed in the distance, and she took in a deep breath.

"No, actually I'm not."

"Well, that explains everything. Why didn't you mention that before?"

"He thinks I'm still married."

Elsa held the phone from her ear, as Margot went into a rant about Charles, the son of a bitch, and how Elsa had to let go and move on, which ended by Margot saying, "Oh, the hell with it. What do I know? But Elsa, at least tell me you're going to sleep with him."

"He could possibly have a girlfriend." Olga's sweet smile and almond eyes flashed in her mind.

"Well, find out. What are you waiting for?" Margot said with impatience.

In the afternoons, after a short siesta, Elsa usually took out her journal and books. Instead of emails, she wrote letters in longhand to Margot and to her parents. That afternoon, as she lay on her bed, she noticed the same tall shadow pass faintly along the wall, though it appeared less ominous in the soft light. She shuddered. She sensed their presence. Was it Salvatore? Aunt Esther? She knew the shadow was a darker spirit, while the pacing feet and sobbing came from a gentler soul. Elsa had to believe it was merely fantasy to keep her sanity, but a deeper part of her sensed it was true. For some reason, she didn't feel as afraid any more. She mostly felt saddened by their presence.

Elsa's thoughts drifted to her conversation with Margot, and she couldn't shake thoughts of Gustavo–and how he was looking at her the other night. How she had felt like kissing him.

She was so out of practice, and felt insecure with the idea. Elsa put the back of her hand to her lips, letting them soften and moisten to her skin. She closed her eyes and imagined her hand were Gustavo's lips. Hot tears formed in the corner of her eyes, as she kissed the soft skin long and deep. She felt warmth and tingling, and resisted the urge in that moment to touch herself.

Suddenly Elsa opened her eyes, and she knew what she had to do. She went through her clothes, changing into her favorite jeans and blouse. She took a few minutes to tame her curly hair, and dab on a little make-up, before rushing downstairs and calling out, "Meli, I need a taxi *por favor.*"

During the short drive into town, Elsa didn't let herself think or analyze. She focused on the sensation of the kiss. It wasn't long before she was standing in front of the medical center, and that's when the doubt and reality set in. The taxi had already driven off, so she couldn't turn around. Anyway, she figured that Gustavo already saw her through the window.

She stood there waiting, but he didn't come out. She felt paralyzed. What if he was in there with Olga, and what if they were lovers? Elsa would feel so foolish. As she stood there, the heat of the afternoon sun descended on her. Flies began to swirl in front of her, and she noticed a few kids gather a short distance away, covering their mouths as they giggled and pointed at her. Wherever she went, she drew attention. Now she couldn't move.

Suddenly she felt a tap on her shoulder. She jumped, startled, and turned around. Gustavo was standing behind her, smiling in the same relaxed way he always did.

"How long have you been standing there?" Elsa asked, slightly annoyed and embarrassed.

"Not long. But I wanted to see if you were going to open the door," Gustavo said playfully. "But, seriously, I'm very happy to see you again."

"You rushed off so quickly the other night." Elsa said, almost as a question.

"Yes, I guess I should be honest. I felt a strong attraction to you," Gustavo said while looking her in the eye.

Elsa blurted out, "But what about Olga?" She immediately regretted the question.

"Olga?" Gustavo's expression changed to bewilderment.

"I guess I just assumed you were seeing her." Elsa wished she could flee. She felt the weight of uncertainty engulf her.

Gustavo shook his head and chuckled. "Olga has a husband and three children."

"Well, she must be older than she looks," Elsa said meekly.

"I would have told you if it were otherwise, Elsa. I hope you believe that." Gustavo gazed intently into her eyes.

"Well, I guess I should be honest, too. I'm not really married." Elsa felt her face burning. It felt strange making such a declaration.

"I figured as much."

"You did? But why?" Elsa was surprised.

Gustavo nodded once again toward her hand, the hand she had been kissing just a short time ago. "I noticed the other night that you weren't wearing the ring anymore."

Elsa looked down at her hand, realizing that she had forgotten about the wedding ring. She hadn't remembered taking it off. Her lips had grazed so close, and she didn't even notice.

Gustavo continued, "I don't really blame a woman for wearing a ring, I'm sure it makes dealing with men easier. We can be so hard headed."

"I was married, but my husband had an affair. I divorced a year ago, and I'm still adjusting to things. I hope you understand." Elsa could hardly believe the words just spilling out, after she had stayed guarded for so long. She felt proud of herself for being honest, not just with Gustavo, but with herself as well.

"So what now?" Gustavo asked.

"Would you like to have dinner again, tonight?" Elsa asked, returning his look, forcing herself to not turn away out of shyness.

Chapter 7

During dinner that night, Elsa and Gustavo had a long conversation about their favorite books and authors. Elsa told him about having her most coveted literary works sent to her. Her mother had sent one small box of books by post when Elsa explained that there was virtually no other entertainment. She reveled in Woolf, Lawrence, and García Márquez: prose that she could read over and over without tiring, savoring each line while pondering every passage. So later that night, as she and Gustavo sat on the front porch, she opened *Women in Love* and read a passage out loud to him.

After she read, they looked up at the stars together. She felt Gusatvo's arm reach around her and his hand caress her back. She turned to him, and he leaned toward her and they kissed. She had prepared herself for this, but it felt so much better than she even expected. It was gentle at first. There was just a brief moment of awkwardness, as she adjusted to the feel of him, the contour and fullness of his lips. They took their time to know each other, to fall into synchronicity, until finally, she led him by the hand upstairs. She did this without thinking, without analyzing what would happen afterward. Elsa felt sure, after waiting for so long to take the chance. She trusted him.

Charles had a soft, hefty body that had always reminded Elsa of a gentle bear. Now she adjusted to Gustavo's lean, tight body. Elsa felt self-conscious at first. Gustavo slid off her blouse, and she undid her bra. His hands pulled up her skirt and cupped her, while he kissed her neck, her jaw, her chin and then deep on her mouth.

As Elsa fell onto the bed, Gustavo's hands ran along the length of Elsa's body and he looked dreamy-eyed and intoxicated. Perhaps sensing her hesitation, Gustavo whispered to her, "Your curves are so delicious. I could eat you up." Then he licked and nibbled at her soft hips, at her belly and then at her breasts. He took a nipple into his mouth, and Elsa moaned.

It had been so long since she had made love, she was almost frightened by the intense sensation. The pleasure was painful, a deep and aching pain that throbbed throughout her entire body, from her toes to her head. She thought for an instant about falling too deep into the bliss, about losing herself completely and going mad, while hot tears ran from her eyes. When they came together, Elsa felt like they were up in the Milky Way together, flying through the universe, bodiless, weightless, fearless, and totally at one.

Afterward they lay together, entwined and spent, as Gustavo traced the line of her torso with his fingertip. He said, "You are a beautiful woman, Elsa. So beautiful, I can hardly breathe."

"You don't know how much I needed this. Thank you," she replied softly. He leaned over her and kissed her forehead, her eyelids, her lips, but gently like a tiny bird.

"How much longer will you be here, Elsa?" he asked.

"I don't know. But it's getting harder and harder to leave. There's really nothing calling me back, except maybe my job. But I don't know if I want to keep teaching. I don't make much money, and I'm tired." Elsa told him.

She didn't tell him about avoiding Charles on campus, taking the backstairs and using the far parking lot to keep from running into him. How could she have lived that way for the past year? Now she faced the reality that she had wanted to quit her job for a long time, but she just didn't have the courage.

Elsa and Gustavo spent the following days together, hardly leaving the bedroom. Gustavo would run to the clinic in the mornings, but then he'd return promptly. Then they would lie together for hours, making love and talking, sitting on the balcony to watch the sun fall behind the mountains. Elsa vaguely worried about what Meli and Hernán thought of the situation, but they politely kept a distance, making it easier for Elsa to feel discreet.

Even her nighttime ghostly visitors were keeping their distance, and had ceased to appear while Gustavo was there.

One late morning, they sat together on the balcony, sharing a fleshy, aromatic cherimoya fruit. The sweet juice ran down Gustavo's chin, and Elsa leaned over and licked it. He took her hand and gently licked each fingertip. "So sweet," he whispered.

Then he said in a serious tone, "There's something I've been meaning to tell you, Elsa." There was a pause.

Elsa suddenly tightened up, remembering her previous judgments about him as a Latino, suspecting him of having a wife tucked away somewhere. She braced herself.

"I have to go away for a while."

There it was. She should have known it was coming.

Gustavo continued, "I am working with Doctors Without Borders, and we have a mission planned to the Amazon. I've had the trip planned for months, and I know I should have told you sooner. I just didn't want to ruin all this."

Though she hated the idea of him leaving, part of her was relieved it was only that, and not a wife.

"For how long?" she asked.

"Six weeks."

"But what about the clinic?" Elsa could feel herself preparing to protest.

"I already made arrangements with Olga. She's taking over while I'm gone," Gustavo explained.

Her heart sank. If Elsa left for the States, she might never see him again. But what if she didn't leave? What if she quit her job and stayed at Wayi? She had been toying with the idea, thinking about her savings, about renting her cabin to make an extra income, about helping Meli to export the silk, even teaching English at a local school. She could email the administration and resign. Elsa wondered how Gustavo would react to the idea, would it scare him off? Were things moving too quickly between them? But when Elsa proposed the idea of staying longer, Gustavo hugged her to his chest, and they both stumbled to the bed, where they made love and held each other all afternoon.

A week later, they were saying goodbye. Elsa hid her disappointment by telling Gustavo, "Such a noble man working for a noble cause. They are lucky to have you. Just know how much you'll be missed." She didn't want to be needy or clinging. She worked hard to suppress her feelings of abandonment.

"I promise to make it up to you, *mi amor*," he told her tenderly while kissing her neck. She rubbed into him and let the reality sink in. Six weeks. She could surely handle six weeks.

As quickly as Gustavo had come into her life, he was gone. She didn't regret her love for him; it was now something she could cling to night after night. The memory of his caresses, his kisses, his body pressed to hers, sustained her. Elsa began to mentally make plans to move there permanently.

She would fly back to the States to pack and ship her belongings, and say goodbye to old friends. Elsa would carefully box her book collection, by far the most valuable thing she owned, along with her Underwood typewriter. And maybe a few choice pieces of furniture. Then visit her parents, and she would have to see Margot, her dearest friend in the world. Margot would surely come to visit Elsa, once she was settled. She'd visit Aunt Lina and her crooked old house in Lima for a time, before coming here to live. It was all arranged in her mind.

She thought about resigning from the college. Taking that step both terrified and exhilarated her. Really, she should have left the college a long time ago. While sitting in the small, dusty Internet cabin in town, she carefully composed a letter of resignation, and only hesitated briefly before hitting send. Then she emailed Alejandro to explain to her brother her desire to not sell the house right away. She didn't know how he would respond. She surprised herself by taking these decisive steps, but also worried about her impulsiveness. Elsa hoped she wasn't making a huge mistake.

For the time being, she continued to work in the gardens during the day, and at night she dreamed of Gustavo's return. She wondered if the ghosts would reappear; it seemed that Gustavo had frightened them off. At night, while lying in bed, she listened for the pacing feet, she watched for the shadows, but there was nothing.

Once in a while Elsa found herself roaming the house, searching for remnants of the past. She was still curious about the events there, especially about the murder. Elsa wanted to understand what really happened.

One day, Elsa's roaming brought her to Lucía's bedroom. She wanted to find some clues to her great-grandmother's life, so she once again looked through all of the dresser drawers, but they had been cleaned out and emptied after so many years. There was a small armoire against the wall that she rummaged through, finding only a few moth-eaten wool sweaters and an aged, decaying copy of the New Testament.

It seemed strange that there weren't more of Lucía's belongings left behind. At some point the house had been scrupulously cleaned and the clues to Lucía's life were cleared out along with her things. Maybe it was for the best; knowing Elsa's weakness for the influences of her ancestors, a home immersed in memory would have surely overtaken and engulfed her in a past that was, after all, not truly her own.

Exploring the nooks and crannies of the house eventually lost its intrigue, and Elsa was left with an uncluttered, understated home to create and invent upon. Yes, it was better that way. Elsa was able to bring all of herself into the surroundings and mold them to her, not the other way around.

Salvatore and Lucía oversaw preparations for their visitors: clearing the yards, cleaning the house, and stocking the kitchen. As was custom, the neighbors would get together for fiestas honoring the Virgin or a saint, the harvest or a marriage, and also for funerals. The guests would arrive at Acutambo from neighboring haciendas, a good distance away, to stay for a week or more. A caravan could be seen heading down from the dirt road, led by loaded down mules and children scampering up ahead, followed by livestock such as a pig to roast or a calf to slaughter, and numerous servants to tend to the entourage of visitors.

Now the neighbors gathered for Holy Week leading up to Easter. Lucía greeted the arrivals, with José and Angelica by her side, along with Aunt Esther who wore an angry expression. It was apparent that Esther did not like visitors. She was jealous and protective of her domain.

Lucía said, "It's so warm today. If I didn't have you children by my side, I think I would just lift my arms and float away." Angelica took her mother's hand. Eleven-year-old Angelica had flowing, honey blonde hair and bright, piercing eyes.

Angelica was timid around the guests, and frightened by the procession that evening.

In honor of *Maria la Dolorosa*, the Virgin Mary in mourning, there was a funeral procession for Jesus. Everyone dressed in black and walked alongside a coffin symbolically housing the body of Christ. The pallbearers carried the coffin down the dirt road as the women followed alongside, crying into handkerchiefs held to their faces. There was a medley of moaning, wailing, and singing as the procession meandered through the grounds by moonlight until reaching the chapel.

Suddenly, three men on horseback galloped straight up to the crowd and began cursing. Wearing large *sombreros* and scarves over their faces, they rode through the procession, holding up machetes and yelling, "*Gringos*, foreigners! You are thieves in our land. We curse you, and we will take back what is ours."

The women shrieked and some fainted. The crowd went into a commotion. The coffin was dropped to the ground, as people scattered. And then just as quickly as they had appeared, the men rode off into the darkness. One of Salvatore's neighbors stepped to the front of the crowd and demanded that they form a posse to go after the insurgents, but Salvatore discouraged him and tried to settle the mob.

The Indians had never been so worked up. They spent the following days retelling the story. Even Pedro, the foreman of the hacienda, was drawn into the drama of that night and embellished the retelling to include gunshots and the kidnapping of an attractive maiden. The owners of the haciendas now had worries about uprisings and protests by their workforce.

The Plague wasn't about to let Salvatore forget the riotous night. She told him, "Salvatore, you have no control over these natives. If I were in charge, this never would have happened. What we need around here is a man—a real man."

"You are as macho as they come, *Tia*. I could never compete with someone as manly as you," Salvatore said just as his nervous tic kicked in. He blinked hard and quick three times. But then he folded his hands at his waist and gave her a stiff bow.

Esther wasn't sure if she was to take the remark as a compliment or not. She decided that even if he was mocking her, it was flattering to be considered a woman with *huevos*, good size balls, and so she grunted and strode away with a virile swagger. "It should bother you; don't forget that I'm just an old lady. After all this time, you still haven't taken my advice. You're still weak and pathetic," she yelled over her shoulder.

Salvatore stood next to Pedro and glanced at the foreman to see if he had caught the insult. Pedro was scraping dirt from his sandals with a stick, and acted as though he was unaware. Salvatore was angry with the Plague, but even more with himself. She was still able to make him feel like the same boy he was years ago.

One afternoon, Elsa rested in bed while reading a favorite book. Her eyes scanned the room decorated with fresh cut geraniums and sunflowers, ceramic bowls filled with colorful mangoes, papayas and oranges from the garden. She had created something of her own and to her liking. It was simple but charming, and those golden rays began to seep in from the open terrace to fill the room with radiance and warmth.

She looked up at the ceiling and something caught her attention: the door in the ceiling, leading to the attic. It was small and painted over, so she hadn't noticed it before. She noticed the fine black seam outlining the door, and it toyed with her curiosity.

She stood on the bed, reaching up on her tiptoes to push the door open. It didn't budge and Elsa wasn't quite tall enough. She piled up pillows and began to gently jump up and down, and while gaining momentum Elsa pushed with greater force until it suddenly burst open. She saw the dark space through the hole in the ceiling. She pushed the bed to one side and brought over a chair, but still not being tall enough, she called Hernán and Meli to help hoist her up into the attic.

"Be careful, Doña Elsa. Do you want me to go?" Hernán asked.

Meli nodded her head, and said, "Let Hernán go up instead."

Elsa ignored their concern, as she insisted that Hernán lift her with his arms and she stepped into his cupped hands.

Once inside the small space, her eyes adjusted to the darkness and she got goose bumps when she realized the abundant treasure she had discovered. She assumed everything there belonged to her great-grandmother Lucía. There were piles of satin, ruffled dresses with corsets and sun hats adorned with ribbons and lace, stacks of books, and old china dishes with chips and cracks. Elsa opened up a box to find photo albums and letters. A treasure chest of memories and history overflowed and cascaded, ready to drown her in the cramped space. The dust overpowered her.

Meli yelled from below, *"Está bien*? What did you find?"

Elsa answered, "Yes, I'm fine. There are a lot of boxes. Give me a few minutes, please."

Where to begin? She noticed right by her feet a box of lace curtains, and though musty, unfolding one she immediately envisioned it hanging in the bedroom. The curtain was a beautiful, elegant ivory color, delicate but not frilly.

"Here, I'm going to pass you down one box. These are curtains we can use." Elsa lifted the box and leaned down. Hernán reached up and took it from her.

Elsa saw another smaller box nearby filled with photographs and letters folded in envelopes addressed to Lucía, and so she also handed them down to Hernán and Meli who were waiting patiently below.

After a few minutes, Elsa dangled her legs, and they awkwardly guided her back down from the attic. She brushed the dust from her clothes and hair with the back of her hand. She settled herself on her bed, and began to leaf through the papers.

"I'll start washing the curtains, and clean up whatever else I find. *Vámonos*, Hernán." Meli and Hernán left Elsa.

Elsa noticed the smart, sophisticated beauty of another era in the photographs taken decades ago, when women looked chic in stylish hats and the men wore suits as casual attire. She noticed letters handwritten in fine script and quickly skimmed one that she gathered to be written by Angelica to her mother. She savored the subtleties and suggestions written between the lines of those letters. *"Miguel is already learning to walk, and his father is away, missing his first steps… The winter days in Lima are damp and dreary, how I long for sunshine…"*

One photograph slipped from the stack onto the floor, and Elsa picked it up and looked at it. It was a family portrait of Salvatore and Lucía with their children. She recognized the couple from photographs she had seen at the house in Lima.

Salvatore and Lucía had the same sophisticated and handsome air. But then Elsa noticed the woman standing just over Salvatore's shoulder, wearing a black frock and a bonnet. She drew in a quick breath. Elsa knew from the family stories that it had to be Aunt Esther. She was tall and slender, her face was angular and she had dark, beady eyes. She wore a menacing smirk and was looking down at Salvatore. Elsa shuddered at the image of the Plague.

Just then, someone was banging on the front door downstairs, and yelling, "Hernán, Meli, Señora Elsa, come quick."

Elsa quickly placed the photograph and all of the papers back in the box and ran downstairs.

One of their neighbors was at the door, holding Meli's eldest daughter, Ruth, in his arms. The girl was sobbing and holding her arm to her chest.

"I found her down by the creek, she had fallen off a boulder. I think she's broken her arm." The neighbor held the girl out to Hernán, who took his daughter gently and carried her inside. Meli took charge, and with surprising calmness, checked over her daughter's injury. Ruth whimpered softly with her eyes closed.

Elsa rubbed Ruth's head lightly and whispered to her, "You'll be all right, *mi angel.* Everything's all right."

Meli shook her head, and said, "It's not broken—it's sprained. She will be okay. I have good medicine for this." Meli quickly set to work on boiling herbs and wrapping the sprain.

Hernán calmly told Elsa, "There's no need to call Olga. Meli's medicine is just as good."

Elsa spent the next few days poring over old letters and photographs. As she sorted through the photos, she composed a collage of history—a sort of roundabout timeline of faces and places. Sometimes, Elsa was able to match letters to those faces, as she tried to decipher and then organize years and generations. She found an old sepia photograph of her great-uncle, José, in the Amazon surrounded by huts and natives. There was another of Salvatore and Lucía on their wedding day, with Salvatore's rotund mother sobbing into a handkerchief in the background. However, Elsa was most astounded by the picture of Aunt Esther looking down on Salvatore. She found another of Esther holding baby Angelica in her arms. The Plague was truly a frightening image even at her happiest moments.

Elsa was reminded of the family stories: Salvatore's journey from Italy, wise Lucía and their two high-spirited children, Angelica and her brother José, and then later in his life there was Salvatore's second family in Lima.

But Esther's murder was the mystery that remained unsolved. Elsa remembered that her father had said that they all suspected a local Indian had killed her. Yet, Aunt Lina also said that there was never any proof that he did it. Who was the man? Elsa now wondered. Given Esther's cruel treatment of the Indians, it would be no surprise that one of them would seek vengeance. How could anyone ever find out the truth after all these years?

Nemesio's hatred for the European landowners could be traced directly to Esther. He lived out his entire childhood with building resentment, despising her as she rode her black beast through the estate, hurling insults at him. "Work, you stupid, lazy boy," she would shout. And his mother carried a scar on her leg from the infamous horsewhip. He loathed her superior air, the way she looked down on him and his family, and he shivered with rage and humiliation whenever he thought back to the single most degrading, even heartrending, moment of his life.

It had been on one occasion in which Nemesio was discreetly following Angelica through the hacienda, as she made one of her rare appearances. Her father bid her run an errand, and seeing that Esther was overseeing the harvest that morning, Angelica was taking her leisurely time. Nemesio was caught off guard by Angelica's call to him and the sudden invitation to walk alongside her. Although he always followed her whenever he had the opportunity, she had never paid any attention to him before. He trailed in her shadows, feeling invisible, and had gone unnoticed for so long that when she finally spoke to him, actually acknowledging his existence, he found himself speechless, yet completely obedient.

This time he walked right next to her along the dirt road. He was so close to her that he could hear her breathe; he could smell her sweet perspiration and feel a sort of electricity, a warm vibration emanating from her being. The hairs on his arms stood on end, giving him goose bumps. His senses were heightened by the excitement of walking alongside Angelica, the girl he had grown up watching from a short distance. He knew he loved her, had loved her since he could remember.

She hummed while she strolled, and once they arrived at the plaza she stopped short and turned to him. "Would you like some lemonade? I can ask Maria to bring us a pitcher from the house," Angelica asked with all her innocence.

"*Sí, Señorita*," was all he could say as his voice squeaked and he turned the color of boiled beets.

"I know, we can sit right there, under that big tree, and have a cold drink. Wouldn't that be nice?" she said as she trotted over to the shade under the canopy of green leaves.

Nemesio couldn't breathe, and his skin felt like it was being pricked with needles. Angelica laughed at his frightened, boyish expression and the blankness of his stare at her impulsive offer. When she laughed she tossed her head back and opened her mouth, and Nemesio could see all her perfect little teeth. Her eyes sparkled and her hair swayed in the wind, catching sunlight in its strands, weaving a crown of copper upon her head. He sat down next to her, on a patch of grass, keeping a very straight posture and using slow, deliberate movements as if he were trying to catch a wild thing in the brush. Angelica only laughed harder, but strangely he didn't mind. He was concentrating too hard to feel insulted by her impudence.

"Nemesio, I've known you my whole life but I don't recall you ever having said even one word to me. Why is that, why do you pretend to ignore me? I feel you following me, but it seems like you are angry with me. Do you despise me, Nemesio?" Angelica seemed to be taunting him in a playful but curious manner.

The young man seethed with embarrassment, unsure how to respond to the capricious, bold girl sitting on the grass next to him. She continued giggling with harping chirps like a small bird, and smelling of some kind of sweetness, not of citrus in the orchards or of any flower he encountered before.

Angelica leaned over him to pluck a small yellow flower, and Nemesio closed his eyes and then relaxed slightly, allowing a full breath into his lungs and his shoulders to fall back. Just then he felt a sting on the back of his neck. At first he thought it was a bee, and he slapped it with the palm of his hand. But before turning around, he saw the look in Angelica's eyes, a look of horror and surprise, and his entire body froze. He turned around slowly, and everything seemed to be suspended in time.

The Plague stood over him on her dark beast, with whip in hand. He thought he detected a slight smile upon her face, a smirk of vindication, before she began lashing him. "You ignorant fool, I will beat you to death for this!"

She chased Nemesio throughout the grounds, and he ran like a confused, dazed prey being hunted by a predator. He felt trapped, as he ran in circles around the plaza while being tailed by the horsewhip. Angelica ran home crying. Nemesio, finally exhausted, rolled into a fetal position. It took his father and three other men to drag him away, though they got their share of lashes in the process. Esther had never been more savage, she seemed to have truly lost her mind to rage.

Nemesio never spoke to Angelica again, and avoided her as if his life depended on it, which it may have. Angelica felt so sorry and guilty, of course, that she wrote him letters, which were hand delivered to his family's house by Maria. In them, Angelica declared her affection for the young man. *Nemesio, I think you're sweet. I hope you like me, too. Aunt Esther is very mean, I'm sorry. Maybe we can still be friends, I would like that very much. Your friend forever, Angelica.* In the envelopes she put dried flower petals and small pieces of lace, the only things she could think of that seemed romantic and befitting love letters.

Chapter 8

All was quiet at the hacienda. But then, in the dark early morning hours, as all the creatures lay in sweet slumber, a shrill cry was hurled across the valley. The high-pitched, murderous scream, abrupt and intense, was followed by grave silence. Those who were aroused from deep slumber struggled to make sense of two worlds suddenly colliding: the world of the subconscious entangled in dreams and the world of the awake.

Lucía thought she had dreamt the shriek, and it fit best into her world of dreams interlaced with erratic sleep. Lucía tossed herself about until she became aware of lying in her own bed and aware that the strange, awful scream had come from down the hallway. She reached over to awaken Salvatore. Her arm stretched across the bed and her hand flopped around. Realizing he wasn't there, she lifted her head slightly. Lucía called out her husband's name.

Salvatore was already standing in front of the door to Esther's room. He wore a long nightshirt and held a candlestick in one hand, while his other hand rested on the doorknob. The quivering flame of the candle made shadows dance on the wall. Salvatore's entire body was tense and perspiration moistened his brow. He entered and cautiously walked across the room, and the creaking sound of the floorboards grated his bones.

Esther's body was sprawled over the bed. Her eyes stared back at him wide open, bulging with terror. She had a gash in her chest and blood drenched the white sheets and her nightgown. Her hair was a tangled mass.

Salvatore stood motionless near her body, horrified. Salvatore noticed that Esther's gown was bunched up well above her knees, exposing her legs. He blushed when he saw that her legs were slender and muscular. He imagined her fury over this, Salvatore looking at her bare legs, and he was caught in a dilemma. He debated, was it worse to leave her exposed, or risk touching her by lowering the gown? He was so preoccupied with that problem, the fact that she was dead seemed secondary.

Finally he decided to leave her in that compromising position, while he called on the authorities. He closed the door with discretion.

Even though her death incited much talk and speculation, Salvatore was strangely uninterested in pursuing an investigation into the matter. Nonetheless, an officer from Abancay, the closest municipality, came to the hacienda to conduct interviews and search the area.

Salvatore took the officer to Esther's room, and the man examined the bed and opened the dresser drawers and roughly rifled through her clothes. Then he glanced over the rest of her belongings. He laid himself down on the floor to get a look under the bed. When he stood up, he dusted off his uniform.

Salvatore explained, "I don't know what else I can tell you. We all heard the scream, I came into the bedroom, and there she was: a bloody, sprawled mess. *La Pobre*. No one deserves that, not even the Plague." Salvatore held his head with both hands.

"And you don't suspect anyone, *Patrón*?"

"No, no, I can't imagine who could do such a thing."

Then the officer was invited to a cup of tea with Lucía in the sitting room. The gruff official, more accustomed to drinking pisco with his comrades than having tea with a lady, was ill at ease. He held the delicate teacup with both hands and was self-conscious of his muddy boots soiling the fine Persian rug.

"*Señora*, you have no idea who might have wanted to kill your aunt?" he asked.

"Oh my, who would want to murder Esther? She was like a mother to me." Lucía's entire body shook. Although Lucía knew her aunt could be difficult, Esther had been her nursemaid since she was just a baby. Lucía was raised with her aunt's doting attention, so she was blind to Esther's true nature. She was blind to the misery of her husband under Esther's constant abuse.

One night, Elsa was awakened from a deep sleep with a start by loud banging on the window. She jumped up and, though too frightened to approach, she could see masses of small, white figures hit against the glass. The thump and roar was tremendous, as tiny fluttering clumps hit against the pane over and over. Elsa held her breath in terror. She then saw some of the insects fly into the room through the crack in the balcony door. As Elsa sat on the bed, they began to swirl and circle around her. Elsa waved her arms, swatting them away from her head. She tossed her head from side to side and felt the insect wings brush against her cheeks. She covered her eyes and ran to a corner of the room. Elsa calmed herself, as she then realized that they were only delicate, gray moths, who flew frantically until dropping dead to the floor. They were silk moths.

Elsa picked up one of the dead moths, and in the darkness she examined it. It was battered and crushed. It began to fall apart and its wings disintegrated, until completely disappearing from her palm. She glanced over to the door, and once again saw a dark figure move out of sight. Elsa suspected that it was Meli lingering outside the doorway, watching Elsa's struggles with apparitions.

Gustavo had been gone ten days. Being lonely once again, Elsa didn't know if it was her own imagination or if perhaps all the family lore was true. Her father and Aunt Lina certainly had been convinced by Lucía that the house was haunted. She thought about the dark shadow and the quiet sobbing she had experienced since her arrival at the country house.

The following night, Elsa saw him and she let out a cry. His image, no longer hazy and faint, had become clear and vivid to her. After the initial fright, she silently watched, mesmerized by the ghost of Salvatore pacing the balcony and looking over the edge of the railing as if contemplating jumping over. He talked to himself and wrung his hands like a gentle, pacific madman. Had she dreamt it? She thought so until a few nights later. The second time she saw Salvatore in her bedroom, he was kneeling at the foot of the bed, praying and sobbing softly. In the course of a week, Salvatore appeared three times in the middle of the night, always in her bedroom and always in a state of meek torment.

Elsa wasn't afraid of her great-grandfather, because she felt too sorry for him to be afraid. Salvatore never acknowledged her presence; he didn't see her. But Elsa observed him as he muttered to himself, pacing the floor, praying and sobbing. Although it disturbed her to be visited by such a vivid apparition, Elsa continued enduring sleepless nights just to watch him.

On the nights Salvatore wasn't present, another figure began to appear. A benign figure, with a timid demeanor, whispered prayers in Quechua and gesticulated at the foot of the bed. He wore a wool poncho and a knit cap, a *chullo*, woven in deep shades. His eyes flickered with auburn light, and his tawny complexion was testament to his connection to the earth, and Elsa guessed he was the Indian who had been accused of killing the Plague.

Nemesio and Salvatore never appeared together, as if they respected one another's territory in mourning. They existed between worlds, and Elsa felt as if they dwelled in some strange realm of purgatory.

Often times they kept her awake during their visits, but other times she actually dozed off to the rhythm of their weeping and lamenting prayers. The darkness of their remorse and regret was heavy in the room. Elsa felt drawn into a gloomy state.

A couple of nights later, Elsa fell into a restless sleep after reading. She tossed and turned, unable to rest comfortably. She felt too hot, and wondered in her half-asleep state if she had a fever. Suddenly she awakened to the sound of stomping. Rather than the gentle pacing she was growing accustomed to, this noise was loud and caused the entire bed to shake. Elsa searched in the darkness, clutching the blanket around her in terror.

She felt like she was in a dream. Elsa told herself she was when she saw the figure of Esther stomp around the room. Her black satin dress, wisps of gray hair standing on end and her beady eyes depicted a sort of grim reaper.

Elsa groped in the darkness, making her way down the staircase. She slipped on one of the stairs and grabbed the railing to keep herself from falling. She let out a cry. Finally, she made her way into the kitchen and began searching blindly for something. She rummaged drawers and tore through cupboards, grabbing for anything sharp. Instead of a knife, Elsa ended up with a corkscrew in her hand, pointed out in front of her in a defensive position as if it were a sword.

When Elsa regained her senses, she stood trembling, drenched in sweat.

Suddenly, Meli appeared in the kitchen, and gently took Elsa's hand and led her back up the stairs to her bedroom. They didn't speak, but Meli sang quietly in Quechua, just under her breath, "*Qoya waraqwan shaarikurirnin, tsaychawmi kawakullan asikurirnin intita shuyan…*" Her words–rising at dawn, she lives laughing, while waiting for the sun–soothed Elsa as she drifted to sleep again. Elsa woke in the morning with a fever and sore throat.

Meli appeared at her bedside carrying a tray. "I made you tea. You should stay in bed today and rest."

"*Gracias,* Meli." Elsa took a few sips of the chamomile tea and fell back asleep. Her muscles ached, and her head pounded, but she slept. For two days, Meli tended to Elsa, bringing her hot tea, soda crackers and chicken soup, until Elsa regained her strength.

Yet all the while, Elsa yearned to be back home. She thought about her parents, about her cabin, and missed the comfort of her life there. She felt lonely and even afraid. And every night, she found herself tossing and turning, drenched in sweat, fighting off the stomping rage of the Plague.

Once she felt well enough, and exhausted by the frightening apparition, Elsa finally moved into the little room down the hall. There, the nights were quiet, without visitors or ghosts, just the stillness of night. Elsa spent her days on the balcony, but spent her nights in Lucía's little bedroom.

Meli certainly noticed Elsa's move into the other bedroom, but she didn't ask her about it. Elsa had tended the bedding and moved the smaller bookcases herself, and then she began to fill the armoire with her things.

Meli must have been curious, but all she said was, "I hope you like your new bedroom. I'm sure it's cozy."

Elsa had grown fond of Meli, but she had to admit that Meli remained a mystery to her. Meli observed Elsa's struggles with ghosts and life in the mountains with an aloof yet curious manner. She was quick to step in and help, offering a hand when needed, but she seemed detached at the same time. Elsa thought about the iridescent glow from her fingertips, which never washed away, and she still was taken aback at Meli's penetrating, dark eyes whenever their gaze met. Elsa began to wonder what Meli's role might be with the ghostly visitors.

Gustavo had been gone for almost three weeks, and Elsa was counting the days for his return. She had received one letter, which told her about the villages along the Amazon River, and children getting vaccinated for the first time. She was proud of him, though that familiar loneliness crept into her again. Elsa was unsure about a real future with him. Things had moved fast in the beginning, and his departure was so sudden. She was left confused.

Memories of him and the way he fit into her, as if their bodies were molded to one another, tugged at her. His kindness, his gentle but firm presence in both spirit and flesh, left her aching for him on many nights. Yet, she couldn't be absolutely sure of their future together, since everything had happened so fast. She was struggling with the strange haunted house and the growing desire to go home to California. The house was odd and often times frightening, but it also belonged to her. But, really, what was she thinking to stay there? The decision now seemed impulsive and irrational. And Gustavo wasn't there to reassure her.

Elsa decided to call Margot. Her friend was pragmatic, often Elsa's voice of reason. She needed her friend's guidance now.

After small talk, Margot asked Elsa, "So what are your plans, Elsa? Have you set a return date?"

"I had actually thought about moving here, can you believe that? Now I'm thinking I must be mad." Elsa continued to tell Margot about her plans to move there, about her love affair with Gustavo and his sudden departure, but she left out the ghosts. Elsa then asked, "What do you think, Margot?"

"When you said you were going to Peru for a month, I never expected that it would become indefinite. Were you really going to just pack up everything and move there? It would be a rash decision, Elsa. And you're that sure about this guy?"

"You'd understand if you could see it here, Margot. I just got swept away by the magic of this place and by Gustavo. But you're right. It was a crazy idea."

"I don't mean to be so negative. I just miss you." Margot seemed to catch herself. Then she carefully added, "Elsa, I should have told you before but I didn't want to worry you–I've been diagnosed with breast cancer."

Elsa was stunned.

"Margot, how long have you known about this? Why didn't you tell me?"

"There wasn't anything you could do about it, and what good would it have done, just make us both depressed. I'm okay. My sister is helping out with the bookstore and staying with me for now. But, I wanted to tell you because I'm scheduled for a partial mastectomy in three weeks, and then I'll start radiation after that."

Elsa's mind was racing. She had planned on going back anyway, but now she knew it would be sooner rather than later. Elsa began calculating how soon she could get there.

"Margot, I'll be there in a few days."

Elsa wanted to be there for her friend, especially after everything Margot had done for her over the past year during her divorce: offering her extra work at the bookstore even though the place was running on a shoe string, all the late night calls and staying over with her.

"I don't want to worry Kyle. It's his first semester at the university, and this is the last distraction he needs."

"But you told him, didn't you?" Elsa asked.

"Yes, but I told him not to visit until winter break. I can do this, Elsa."

Margot and Elsa had been through a lot, riding the ups and downs of life together. They had seen it all. Elsa realized she had taken Margot for granted. She'd always just been there. Elsa pictured her friend now–with her long, flowing silk skirts and red permed hair.

Elsa had to get back as soon as possible; she knew that Margot needed her. She bought a bus ticket to Lima that very afternoon.

That night, she wrestled with strange dreams. Elsa danced a tango with Salvatore and Nemesio, the two twirling her between them, while Charles watched disapprovingly. Margot grabbed Charles, trying to dance with him and soon they were tangled together, wrestling one another in rage. The Plague looked down on all of them from the top of a staircase, wearing a long black satin dress with ruffles, and she stormed down with a horsewhip in hand.

The room became crowded and the dance became a mad frenzy to escape. In her dream, Elsa rushed out the door and was suddenly with Gustavo on a raft, and they floated peacefully down a river. A slithering anaconda appeared, wrapping its muscular, smooth body around her and squeezing until Elsa woke up gasping for breath. She tried to shake off the feeling that it was a bad omen.

The next day, Elsa found Meli and Hernán working on the patio, sorting through the vegetable harvest Hernán had brought in that morning. Elsa got on her knees, and began shucking corn.

"I want to tell you that I'm leaving in a couple of days," Elsa said while the three worked together.

The couple was quiet for a long while, until Hernán finally said, "I'm sorry you're leaving us."

Elsa looked up and locked eyes with Meli. Elsa couldn't read the expression in Meli's eyes, but there was the familiar penetrating depth in her gaze.

"My friend is sick, and she needs my help. I don't know if I'll be able to come back any time soon." Elsa felt a deep sadness with those words.

Meli and Hernán looked at each other, and they paused their work. Elsa knew they were waiting for an explanation about the decision with the property, about their future there.

Elsa said, "I haven't made any decisions with the house, so for now, you can continue to live here. I'll give you the same salary that my grandmother paid you for taking care of the estate."

They couple nodded their heads, and continued their work in silence.

Elsa spent the rest of the day organizing her things. She took a break in the afternoon to rest on the balcony, taking in the beauty of the mountains for one last time. Elsa had taken the old box of letters and memorabilia with her outside. She sat in the warmth and read through more of the letters. While reposed in a chair, she randomly picked up another yellowed envelope, carefully slipping a fragile, thin paper from its heart. Elsa began to read.

June 23, 1956

My Dearest Wife Lucía,

I have wanted to write this letter to you for many years. It seems as though a thousand times I attempted it, only to let my cowardice win over and the pen and paper fall to my side. Yet, I am driven by torment and grief to a degree far outweighing what a man can survive. So, this letter is written to you out of desperation, not courage.

Looking back over my life, I admit to happiness despite the flaws of my character. Acutambo was my blessed domain, and you beautiful Lucía and our children were the family that sustained me, even with the unnamed yearnings and profound loneliness condemned to marked souls, such as I.

I was one of those marked with a destiny to suffer even amidst blessings.

The thorn of my existence was your aunt, the Plague—entrenched in my world for some inexplicable reason--and her demise has been my cross to bear. What is a man to do when his mortal sins are so heinous and also completely irreparable? What's done is done; no amount of repentance is great enough to erase it from truth. I will forever live with the weight of sin, and I am powerless to change the horrifying likelihood that I am destined to pay with eternal damnation for a single act committed in this lifetime.

Before my death, I owe an apology to all of the people involved in my treachery. To you my sweet wife and to our children for having such a shadow cast on our family name; and Pedro's family, and his son Nemesio, for having to endure my betrayal. My sin, being so profound, I'm afraid will never be absolved.

Pray for me Lucía, pray for me the rest of your days on Earth and from Heaven too, upon your own passing to that holy realm. Remember me always, so that one day I may be freed. When I depart from this earth, don't mourn me—only pray for my decrepit soul.

Your adoring husband,

Salvatore

Elsa reread the passages in the letter, examining each faded word to make sure she wasn't mistaken. She thought about Salvatore's second family, and how he had hid it from Lucía and his children until his death. That was certainly a betrayal. Yet, she continued to read the letter ten times over before she wrapped her mind around the truth. When the full realization of her great-grandfather's crime settled on her, she gently placed the letter onto her lap.

Elsa absentmindedly stroked the lifeline on the palm of her hand with the tip of her finger, as she gazed out over the shimmering green fields spread before her. She had just discovered that Salvatore murdered Esther. She thought about what this meant to her and her family. Lucía obviously knew about her husband's crime, but she had chosen not to tell the family.

After her aunt's murder, Lucía moved to the capital with her family. Her marriage didn't survive, and then Salvatore got cancer. After his death and once her children were grown and married, Lucía moved back to the country house. She hid the confession from her family.

Elsa sat on the balcony, contemplating the bitterness of life and the desperation we all carry deep within us. The grisly murder disturbed her wellbeing. And she asked herself what she should do with this information. Did Angelica want her to reveal the secret to her family? She couldn't bear the thought of telling her father that his grandfather was a murderer, but there could be no other option.

Chapter 9

Nemesio had been walking through the grounds under a full moon. He was startled when he saw Don Salvatore down by the creek. Nemesio crept closer and saw his *patrón* rinsing out his shirt and washing his dark-stained hands in the current. Nemesio watched then as Salvatore kneeled by the water's edge, sobbing and retching while thrashing himself against the rocky knoll.

Nemesio tried to sneak away, but he stepped on a pile of dry debris. Don Salvatore jumped to his feet, and seeing that it was his young field hand, he ran to him. *El Patrón* cried out, "Nemesio, the Plague is dead. Everyone saw what she did to you in the plaza, that day she whipped you for following Angelica through town. They'll think you are guilty, no matter what I tell them. Run boy, run into the mountains and never return or you will hang for Esther's murder." And that's just what the boy did.

Nemesio was only fifteen years old when he left the hacienda in the middle of the night without a word to anyone, not even his own father. Once he reached the highlands, he tried to gather the Indians together for meetings, and with salty tears in his eyes and a red-flushed face, he preached to them about an uprising.

"The white men, they call us burros. They think we're as stupid as donkeys. They take our land and call it their own. I say we fight and take back what's ours."

"What do we fight with?" a man asked Nemesio. He was as old and crooked as a quenual tree, and his hands and feet were black from soot.

"Machetes, pistols, knives, whatever you have."

"Hmm, I've never seen a pistol but I do have a machete. I use it to cut firewood."

"That's good."

"But, if I use the machete for *la revolución* then what will I use to cut firewood?"

"You won't cut firewood while you're fighting."

"But then how will my family eat?"

"*Ay, Viejo*! We'll figure that out later!"

The old man was not impressed. Anyway, his family had lived on the same land since only God knew when, and nobody ever bothered them about it.

The Indians gathered to hear Nemesio's impassioned speeches, more out of curiosity and a break from the monotony of their uneventful days, than from true commitment to his cause. They listened to his leftist sermons with mild interest, passing the bottles of *chicha* around as they chewed on wads of coca leaves. The ball of leaves were then tucked in their cheeks and as they trekked home from the meetings, miles up into the remote highlands where a hut awaited them filled with children, smoke, and guinea pigs roasting in the wood oven.

Elsa was ready to leave for California. Since her decision to leave Peru, she had sent two emails from the Internet cabin in town to let Gustavo know. Though he told her that Internet access would be intermittent, she still waited anxiously for his reply. Elsa hated to admit that she harbored a fantasy that he would come running back to her. Just as she boarded the bus he would appear, at the last moment, falling to his knees to claim is undying love for her.

Instead, she received an email telling her that he was sad and disappointed that he wouldn't be able to see her off. He was working in a small village near the Brazilian boarder. He wanted assurance that she was coming back to Peru, but Elsa didn't know how to answer him. She had told him about Margot's cancer, but she left out her doubts about returning by telling him that as soon as he was back, they would talk about future plans. Her disappointment in not seeing him in person to say goodbye felt crushing. She also felt worried. Did he really want her to come back? They were just getting to know each other, build a relationship, when it was torn apart by his leaving. How serious was it, Elsa questioned.

The morning of her departure, Elsa sat on the back porch watching the children play with the dog. They had tied a rope around him like a harness, and the youngest was trying to ride the mutt like a horse. The dog just went around in circles trying to bite his own tail. Hernán was approaching from a morning of work in the fields, and Elsa watched him as he limped along slowly. His contentment was obvious but discreet, held within the center of his being. She was leaving that afternoon, but for now the sun rose overhead and she took in the day with serenity, saying prayers for Margot.

Hernán stopped short of approaching the porch, and stood under a large avocado tree. He leaned against the trunk and began to pick the dirt out of his boots with a stick. He glanced up every now and again at her, and then Elsa understood that he was waiting for her to go to him.

Elsa approached him casually, kicking up her heels like a child as she walked over the soft grass. She stood under the shady canopy with Hernán, and he politely removed his straw hat before speaking to her.

"Mamá Elsa, I know you are leaving tonight. Everything will be left in good hands, you can be assured," he said in less than perfect Spanish. His accent was distinctive to the Indians who learn Spanish as their second language. His accent actually sounded a lot like Elsa's, mixing up the vowels in the same manner.

He continued, "I've been waiting for the right time to talk with you. Now that you are leaving soon, this is a good time. I'm sorry, and maybe it doesn't even matter, but I think you should know. My grandfather had a history with your family."

Elsa was curious. "What do you mean, Hernán?"

"There were accusations."

"What is your grandfather's name?"

Hernán hesitated a moment. In almost a whisper, he replied, "Nemesio."

Elsa almost fainted.

She immediately wondered if that was the reason for the family's coldness toward her.

Hernán began to tell her the same stories that were told to him.

Hernán rubbed the straw hat between his hands as he spoke. "I was told that my grandfather was a witness to the murder, well practically a witness." He added, "My grandfather lived with such hatred and resentment that he couldn't even be sure, as time went by, that he was innocent of the crime. Sometimes our truths can get muddled."

Hernán continued, "Doña Lucía tried to cleanse this house once, after Don Salvatore died. Angelica was married with children and visiting from the capital. I was fairly young then, but I remember it well." Hernán explained this to Elsa in his hypnotic, rhythmic voice.

Lucía had called for a priest from Abancay; Padre Francisco de Velasco was a Basque from Spain. He came to the house, dressed in black except for the white priest's collar, and he carried a small black leather case.

"Oh, thank you, Father, for coming all the way here. We've been so anxious for your arrival. As I told you, this house is in need of a blessing." Lucía spoke with urgency holding the priest's hands.

Angelica was in the throes of raising her children. She was strong and energetic. She nodded her head and added, "I've been trying to talk my mother into this for a while now. She was so stubborn. But I say, a little holy water never hurt anyone—except someone that you don't want hanging around."

"Don't worry, we'll just have a little stroll through the house and say some prayers. Shall we?" Padre Francisco said with a lisp, spraying spit. He was pale and rubbed his stomach with a pained expression.

"Do you feel all right, Father?" Lucía was nervous, and she noticed that his lips were dry and chapped. "Can I offer you a refreshment?"

"Oh no, *mi hija*. I don't recommend eating ceviche in the sierra. I should have known better than to eat raw fish this far from the coast."

He opened the leather case and inside were his implements: a polished silver and wood crucifix, a small bottle of holy water, and a hand-sized bible. Lucía and Angelica had remembered to buy white candles for the ceremony. The candles were passed out to everyone present, some neighbors and a few friends. Already the priest was beginning to sweat, and they hadn't even begun.

"Padre, I hope you don't mind, but I have some extra holy water that I saved from the Mass of the Resurrection. May we use it too?" Lucía brought over a tin which had once held olive oil, and poured some of the water into a glass jar.

It had been blessed at the four-hour long Mass. The parishioners were allowed to bring their own water, which they carried in dented tin drums, used plastic soda bottles and scraped-up buckets. There was nothing fancy or sacrosanct about the vessels, which sat beneath the altar during the ceremony. Then everyone lugged the containers home, to be saved for special occasions, such as a family member traveling, an evil eye cast at a baby, or an illness.

Angelica picked a yellow Early Sunrise flower from the garden and placed it in the jar of holy water.

"Very well, then. Let's use your water for the blessing," the priest replied.

The priest placed the crucifix over his neck. He held the bible under one arm, and used the flower to spray holy water over the home. He sprinkled the water in doorways, over the bed downstairs, along the bottom of the staircase, in the kitchen and finally over the family members present. He did this while muttering prayers in Latin, which Lucía could barely hear.

When it came time to climb the stairs, he hesitated. "I feel a bit winded, light-headed from the fish, you know." He was pale, his lips a shade of blue with yellow crust caked at the corners of his mouth, and he was panting.

"I'm so sorry to inconvenience you, Father. But please, the upstairs needs your blessing. It is important." Lucía whispered in a pleading, desperate manner while clutching his arm. "Here now, I'll help you up the stairs."

They walked as a pair up the creaking wooden stairs—the priest supporting his weight on Lucía while she limped, being rather petite in comparison to his stout figure. They walked arm in arm, both tottering heavily up the stairs.

The group strolled through the bedrooms, and just like before, the priest sprayed the water in the doorways and over the beds. Lucía held her breath; she was nervous that some sort of sign would appear—a bad omen or a ruckus—to scare off the priest. But, she was relieved when nothing out of the ordinary happened. They made their way slowly back down the stairs, and Lucía invited Father Francisco to stay for lunch.

"Thank you my child, but as you know, I am not well." He left them shortly thereafter, and Lucía was left with doubts.

"I'm not so sure that worked, Angelica. It seemed too easy, and there was no sign—nothing. Father Francisco was too weak, I don't think he was the man for a job like this."

Lucía wondered if he wasn't a true believer, in the way one needed to be to face The Plague. Lucía was pretty sure that Esther would just laugh at the poor, feeble man. Priest or no priest, he was no match for the ghost of the Plague.

During the car ride back to Abancay, Father Francisco had to pull over to the side of the road several times to vomit the spoiled fish churning in his stomach.

After finding out about Hernán's connection to the family, Elsa was left with a sense of intrigue and also sadness. Each family story was like a puzzle piece, and she had to work hard to make them join and fit. His tale had an odd, irregular shape but it was a significant piece, which made the larger picture much clearer to see.

Hernán gazed thoughtfully into Elsa's eyes, watching her expression. For an instant, Hernán and Elsa's eyes locked and she perceived a strange, misty depth in his dark eyes. She realized then that he knew about everything: plagues and curses, ghosts and murder. Elsa thought that maybe he was given the job of caretaker by Angelica as a sort of compensation for the wrongs committed against his grandfather.

Elsa had to tear herself away from Hernán; she only had an hour left before boarding the bus to Lima. She had already packed, and so that gave her some time to contemplate her goodbye. Elsa strolled one last time through the gardens and then the house and felt uncertainty overcome her once again.

Anyway, she still tried to convince herself, even if half-heartedly, that she would be back one day. Elsa asked the three children, "*Niños*, I'll be back, but I'll miss you terribly. What would you like me to bring you from the U.S. when I visit again?"

The children tumbled and squirmed over her like excited puppies.

"Chocolate!" they all said in unison. Hershey was a delicacy.

"Yes, of course, and I'll bring you lots of other treats." Elsa had a list in mind: new shoes, underwear, socks, clothes galore, toothbrushes with Disney characters, toys and picture books. She planned to bring them loads of presents, necessities really, that most American children took for granted. She wanted to see their faces. And for Meli: new clothes, shoes, perfumed lotions and shampoos. Hernán: novelties like a Swiss army knife, binoculars, a flashlight—toys for a grown man.

Of course, Elsa didn't want to change the contentment they had for the simple things in life; she didn't want to create necessities where they didn't exist. But she knew the fun they'd have. And truthfully, it made her sad to see the children wear the same worn clothes and Meli exchange one simple tattered garment for another day after day. Angelica had paid them a decent salary, but there weren't many commodities in the Andes.

"Be sure to take good care of Volga, kids." Elsa thought it amusing that they named the dog after the Russian river, which they had seen in a faded picture on the 1982 calendar still hanging in the bodega in town.

"Doña Elsa, when you come back, I'll let you iron." Meli kissed her cheek and made the sign of the cross on her forehead.

"*Gracias, Meli. Gracias por todo.*" Elsa had grown attached to Meli, despite Meli's reserve, and she gave her a long hug.

Finally, Elsa rushed to get to the bus station on time. It was a dry, dusty stop a little way down the road, so she walked there with Hernán.

He said, "We'll pray for your safe trip and *que Dios le bendiga.*" He gave her an airy, weightless hug.

The trip was overnight, so Elsa could sleep almost the entire way to the capital, as it cut straight through the most remote countryside.

She noticed the plush and comfortable interior of the liner, and then the diverse population of locals filing into the bus. Some were in traditional dress, women in full skirts and felt hats, holding rosy-faced, brightly dressed children. There were businessmen with humble demeanors carrying shabby briefcases and farmers with bundles of produce to sell at market. The rustic travelers seemed out of place sitting in the velvety, plush purple seats, reminiscent of a casino nightclub.

Elsa sat down in an empty seat and politely nodded to the older gentleman sitting rigid and formal next to her. He was wearing threadbare, faded pants and a white dress shirt. She was touched by his crisply ironed shirt, tucked into his pants and buttoned to his neck, though it wasn't uncommon to see such pride in appearances, despite the conditions of poverty in which many lived. He wore his dusty sandals over callused, blackened feet.

As they sat silently side by side, a homesickness and nostalgia washed over Elsa: homesickness for California, and for Peru even though she hadn't left yet. Thoughts of Margot came to her. She was worried about her, and she silently said prayers for her friend's health.

Then the bus pulled out slowly and swayed over the potholes in the road as if they were on a large ship. She hadn't been in such a comfortable seat in ages, so Elsa reclined and closed her eyes, preparing herself for the long hours that lay ahead.

It soon darkened into nighttime hours, and she sensed the gentle hum of the engine as a faint vibration while the bus cruised along a stretch of highway. She looked out the window into the complete and utter blackness of the night, noticing there was no moon, even the stars were obscured in the void outside. Elsa dozed off.

Chapter 10

When she awoke, it was to a torpid wave of confusion. Strangely, the bus had come to an abrupt stop in the middle of the road, and she noticed the glow of the headlights casting an unnatural aura outside the window. The bus driver scrambled about, while yelling at the people toward the front. The passengers were befuddled and lethargic, and she looked at her watch. It was two o'clock in the morning.

As several ominous figures filed into the bus, Elsa looked around her and took in a deep breath to be sure that she was awake. The men were dressed in fatigues with black scarves tied over their faces and were carrying large rifles. One of the assailants stood rigidly at the front of the bus next to the now vacant driver's seat.

The figure at the front of the bus yelled at the frightened busload, "*Todos quietos y nadie se mueve.*" Elsa's mind raced as she watched them work their way down the aisle, stopping to interrogate and collect valuables from each person in every row. They grabbed at the jewelry first then took wallets and purses from the trembling, mute passengers.

The only thing Elsa could focus on was the bandit beginning to approach her row—everything else was fading and she couldn't think clearly. Elsa clutched her earrings and realized they were worthless, her watch a cheap imitation; she had known better than to travel with expensive jewelry. Elsa rummaged through her daypack and fumbled for her wallet. She was planning to withdraw cash in Lima, and now she wondered if they would accept a bankcard out there in the middle of nowhere.

Elsa knew that if she were in the city they would kidnap and hold her hostage until her funds ran dry. It had become common practice in Lima to kidnap victims, taking them every day to the ATM machine to withdraw the daily limit until their bank account was emptied. It could take days, or weeks, for some even months. But out there on the desolate road, in the middle of nowhere, what would they do with a debit card? She counted a scant fifty-seven soles, which was not even twenty dollars. Elsa's only items of value were the Nikon digital camera, which she clutched in her arms as though it had the power to save her life, and her American passport, which was worth a fortune on the black market but that she felt might also get her killed.

Elsa held her breath as the thief approached her row of seats. The older man sitting next to her had been so still and quiet, he almost made himself invisible. However, the thief spoke to him first. She saw the thief's eyes dart back and forth between the old man and her, so that Elsa was sure he was assessing the situation, realizing he had a *gringa* next in line and all the advantages that could present. She was overcome by a tightening in her chest then a wave of nausea.

Elsa wondered if they might separate her from the rest of the passengers. They might single her out and even rape her out of resentment, ideology, or just for being different. She looked up at the intimidating figure standing over her with the black scarf over his face, and, rather than keep her eyes down, for a moment she felt compelled to examine him.

How surprising, he was so young and slight of build, his tattered tee shirt hung loosely on his thin frame. Even though his face was covered, she could see that he was just a boy. Elsa noticed the perspiration around his brow as he collected the dirty, miserable soles from the old man. The old man even gave him coins, which the boy threw on the floor of the bus, scattering them in all directions. Then she imagined the pathetic, ragtag group of passengers rummaging through their belongings for something, anything of value, handing over the little money they had.

The passengers remained calm. Elsa could hear faint whimpers and baby cries, but it was mostly quiet, whereas the agitation of the thieves mounted, as they began to realize the meagerness of their raid. The boy's dark, bulging eyes gave him a demonic look. When she handed over her coin purse, he snatched it out of her hand. He leaned in closer, pulled her hair and jerked her head backward.

"*Qué mas tienes, gringa*? What else do you have?"

She pointed at her watch, and took it off her wrist with slow, deliberate movements. Elsa handed it over, hoping he wouldn't realize it was worthless–costing only $15.95 at Target. He didn't examine it at all before sticking it in a duffel bag he carried on his shoulder. The bag was still practically empty, dangling loosely off his shoulder and he was more than half way through the bus.

"*Qué mas?*" He yelled at her again, the red of his eyeballs turning an even darker crimson. Elsa's scalp still burned where he had yanked her hair, and then the stench of his breath reached her, turning her stomach as she fought down the bile rising in her throat. Alcohol seeped from his body, engulfing the small, enclosed space with the rancid vapor of cheap booze. Elsa envisioned him, along with his comrades, forcing down rum and cocaine before ambushing the bus.

The old man leaned forward, and Elsa thought he was going to be sick or maybe pass out. Instead, he turned his head and looked at Elsa, and for a brief instant their eyes locked. The old man's eyes were strangely vacant. Elsa sensed him to be an empty shell, which scared her almost as much as the boy standing over her. It was as if the old man had left his body, and his spirit roamed the surrounding pampas outside.

She fumbled for her camera, the one thing she thought might satisfy the bandit. He grabbed it from her violently, stuffed it into the bag. Then he shouted, "Hand over your passport!"

Just then he was distracted as another member of his posse belligerently boarded the bus. He bellowed while waving a large machine gun into the air. He marched down the aisle ordering everyone to get off, which caused panic. Some passengers rushed to the exits while others cowered and cried in their seats.

Elsa made her way to the exit, while the young thug nudged her along with his gun to her back. Thoughts of her father and his warnings beat down on her, and she felt a deep pain for her parents. The love and concern they had for her flooded back.

She scanned the people around her; all of them were terrified. Outside, the bus driver was lying on the ground with a man standing over him. Amidst the confusion, a couple, brave or desperate souls, took their chances by fleeing into the wilderness off the side of the road. Everyone else waited for instructions from the disorganized group of bandits.

While the hijackers argued amongst themselves, disagreeing on the next step to take, the artificial glare of the headlights gave an eerie strobe light effect on the surroundings. The curious white glow seemed to be taunting Elsa. All around her was a deep void of darkness while the light was a beacon, but also alien and ghostly.

Real life can resemble a dream so much at times that all of matter and solid surroundings seem to quiver, then nearly disintegrate in form. Elsa's strange and vivid perception mingled with the headlights of the bus, and the utter darkness along their periphery.

The passengers were forced to the ground to lie on their stomachs with their hands on their heads. Elsa was still trying to be inconspicuous, shrinking herself before the situation. She laid herself out, on her stomach, just like everyone else.

They remained on the ground while the bandits removed the luggage. The thieves tore through the bags, scattering personal effects on the side of the road. They had been pushed to careless measures; it wasn't long before another bus was visible across the dark passageway. The headlights from the other bus, approaching from such a distance, looked like a mirage. Elsa felt one of the bandits standing over her, and she felt the butt of his gun digging into the center of her back. She held back cries of pain.

When the other bus finally arrived, the bandits may have sensed that their raid had run dry, and they would be taking an added risk with more people. They ran and disappeared into the dark desert hillsides of the pampa. Then a military patrol showed up, and while still in shock, the passengers were interviewed quickly and quietly. Eventually they were transported to Lima.

From Lima, Elsa flew directly to San Francisco and then caught a flight to Eureka. She was in a blank stupor. She didn't eat, drink, sleep, or even hardly move during the entire ten-hour journey. She left a voicemail to Margot, telling her the new arrival time but nothing more.

Margot picked her up from the airport. When Elsa saw Margot emerge from the car, wearing a long flowing skirt, her red hair like a halo around her gentle face, Elsa collapsed into her friend's arms. She couldn't hold back the sobs.

"Oh my God, Elsa. Are you okay? What the hell happened?" Margot hugged Elsa tightly, stroking her head with one hand.

Elsa couldn't speak. She cried like she had never cried before. She cried when Charles left her, but that seemed trivial compared to the uncontrollable burst of emotion, driven by fear, and by overwhelming relief.

They stood on a median at passenger pick-up, Margot's car blinking hazard lights. A policeman approached them, waving his arms from side to side and blowing a loud whistle. Elsa still clung to Margot.

"Sweetie, you're scaring me. Just tell me you're all right. And let's get in the car, so you can explain what happened." Margot tried coaxing Elsa.

Elsa wiped away the wetness on her face with the sleeve of her blouse. Her face was splotchy and swollen.

Margot reached into the glove box and then handed Elsa tissue. "Here, use this. Let's get out of here. I'm taking you home," Margot urged.

As they drove to Elsa's cabin, Elsa explained to Margot the whole ordeal. She told her about the dark highway, the bandits wearing scarves and carrying guns, and about lying on the side of the road, all the while believing she would be killed.

"I can't believe this. I think you'll have to talk to someone, Elsa. I mean a professional. You know, for PTS, or something like that." Margot was now pulling the car into Elsa's driveway.

Elsa looked at the cabin that had been empty for two months, her refuge once upon a time, surrounded by gargantuan ferns, trees like pillars of a cathedral, and the pungent scent of organic decay. Elsa had always felt connected to an ancient world there. She walked up the old, rotting steps damp from the rain, and when she went inside the emptiness of the space felt cool and numbing. Margot followed silently behind her.

"I think I need to lie down, Margot. I'm not feeling well." Elsa suddenly ran to the bathroom and vomited, purging the queasiness and dizziness she had felt the entire trip back to the States.

Margot stood in the doorway. "I'm going to make you tea."

Margot tried to convince Elsa to stay with her at her house, but Elsa refused. Deep down, Elsa didn't want to burden Margot, knowing she had enough of her own worries and hardships.

"But we can help each other, Elsa. It's not a burden," Margot explained as they sipped mint tea. Margot had made a fire in the fireplace, and warmth and color was filling the cold, musty space of the living room that had been closed up for so long.

"Let me get settled, and then maybe I'll change my mind." Elsa still felt shaky and weak.

"Will you still go back to Peru, Elsa?" Margot dared to ask nearly in a whisper.

Tears once again ran down Elsa's face, as she said, "I really don't know."

"I shouldn't have asked you so soon. I'm sorry." Margot reached over and took Elsa's hand. Then Margot helped Elsa make the bed with clean sheets and dust off the furniture.

Elsa got settled after a few days, but the memories of the hijacking haunted her at night. She battled her worst nightmares of being shot, of dying on the side of the highway alone and far away from all her loved ones. In the still night, with the lights of the hallway casting long shadows in the room, all of Elsa's fears would surface and there was nowhere to hide.

One night her mind drifted to another traumatic event. She was still with Charles then; they were celebrating their first wedding anniversary.

They had been visiting his parents in Southern California, and were driving up the scenic coastal highway en route to their northern county home. They decided to stay a couple of nights in Big Sur to celebrate their first year of married bliss in one of those romantic, rustic cabins tucked into the spectacular redwood forests hovering above rocky coastal cliffs.

It was pitch-dark as they drove along the winding, two-lane US1 when they saw the headlights of a car. Elsa noticed the odd tilt of the lights and realized they were off the road. As they neared and slowed down, they could see that the car had veered off the road, sideswiped a tree and run straight into a gully.

Charles and Elsa both got out of the car and approached the crashed vehicle. There was a girl by herself, and she rolled down her window. Charles asked her if she was all right, but they could tell she was disoriented, maybe even in shock. She was pale and her lips a grayish shade of blue.

She told them, "I can't move my neck or feel my legs. Help me, please."

There was no cell phone signal, and so Charles said reassuringly, "I'll go wait on the road for someone to pass by. Wait with her, Elsa, and I'll stop the first trucker I see."

Elsa sat with the girl for what seemed like hours, while she remained very still in the driver's seat. They got to know each other as Elsa tried to comfort her, but Elsa was also afraid Jennifer might die that night.

Eventually an ambulance arrived. They took the girl away and Elsa sobbed for two hours without stopping. As it turned out the girl's injuries weren't too severe; Jennifer had whiplash, three fractured ribs, and a concussion.

Now the question tormented Elsa: why did this violence on the bus happen to me? And it was just as her life looked more optimistic and hopeful. She was thankful to be alive, but she felt paralyzed with fear. Doubt and insecurity came at her, riding on endless waves of desperation. Finally she realized that to overcome this, she would have to focus on helping Margot. Her friend needed her.

Elsa sat in the waiting room as Margot was prepped for surgery. The doctors believed they had caught the lump early enough to avoid chemo, but after the partial mastectomy, she would have six weeks of radiation treatments.

Pain, therapy, hospital stays, and operations were things Elsa never imagined occurring to a free spirit like Margot. They had gone to Grateful Dead concerts together, dancing wildly to Jerry Garcia, they had camped in the mountains, and traveled to remote areas in Mexico. She and Margot didn't belong in sterile, artificial hospital wards.

"My God, Elsa, I never would have imagined. Look at me, will you! Breast-less–but not lifeless." Margot laughed behind her tears. Then she winced from the pain.

"You are going to be just fine, and you are so brave," Elsa told her friend. She kissed her on the forehead.

While Margot was sleeping, in recovery from her operation, Elsa snooped around the different hospital wards. She sneaked into the maternity ward, and watched the newborns behind glass walls, which filled her with that old familiar grief. Elsa still longed to be a mother one day.

The geriatric unit was depressing and sad. Elsa yearned to connect to those delicate, fragile people. She played checkers with a scruffy curmudgeon, and then watched TV with silent, over- medicated ladies.

As she sat with them, watching an episode of the 'Golden Girls,' with Betty White making some dingbat joke, one of the ladies leaned toward Elsa. The lady was wrinkly and pale, with her short silver-yellow hair sticking up stiffly around her face. Her lips, dry and gray, moved but no words came out. Elsa leaned in closer to the woman.

"Who is that lady that follows you everywhere?" the patient uttered with a croak, as if her vocal cords had become rusty from disuse.

"My friend Margot just had surgery. She's in recovery."

"Not her, the other one. The older woman with those pretty blue eyes and hair like silk." The patient had a dazed look in her eyes, but then she turned and pointed weakly behind Elsa. Her dry mouth could barely turn a smile, but her eyes had a sparkle of recognition for an instant before clouding over once again. Then she lost herself to the bantering of the lively old ladies on the television screen.

Elsa looked over her shoulder and stared at the sterile, cold room and down the fluorescent lit corridor facing her—feeling for a brief moment like it was the tunnel of light which appears at death—and shuddered.

Of all her father's eccentric family tales, whether real or invented, or maybe just embellished upon as all good stories are, the story of Lucía's brother, Elsa's great-uncle José, seemed the most romantic.

As a young man, José meandered through the open range of the Andes on his thoroughbred mare with a golden mane, the love of his life, for months lodging in villages where he was treated with a respectful disdain, for his pale eyes and fair skin made him a foreigner in his own homeland.

He worked his way eastward, toward the spectacular mountainous jungle with ridges and crests drenched in lush green. He pushed further east, until finally reaching the flat expanse and botanic wonder of the Amazon rainforest. There he discovered entire villages constructed on stilts, tribes with painted faces and naked bodies, chocolate rivers winding like great anacondas, and thick, moist air that suffocated him in his sleep.

In a remote tribal village in the Peruvian Department of Madre de Dios, 'Mother of God,' the small community of Indians rattled in an unfamiliar dialect. Although he was fluent in Quechua, this language reminded him of insects buzzing and chirping in the trees. Some spoke in a slow, muddled Spanish, as if speaking with a mouth full of food, and he began inquiries into the caucho industry.

As a businessman, José was too impulsive and distracted. He was an adventurer at heart. So instead of settling down, he made several expeditions into the deepest parts of the rainforest. With an Indian guide or two, he spent weeks at a time exploring the terrain, taking precise notes and making sketches of his discoveries. He was far from a formally educated ecologist or biologist, but it was a hobby that developed into an obsession. He drew maps as he trekked, collected specimens, and kept a journal for no particular ambition other than to pacify his curiosity.

Decades later, he would have the distinction of having a river named after him. It had taken him several days to stumble upon the wide but shallow brown river carrying debris of leaves, twigs and branches on its mild currents. Then after many years, he would lead a team of government surveyors into the same territory and the river was officially mapped and named Santos.

Shortly after reaching the jungle, he settled in a small village. That's when he spied her, and although she was already engaged to another, he was captivated. He was enthralled by her perfect bare breasts, by her long black hair and serious eyes, and by her dark skin, caramel-colored like his mare, Gypsy. While he serenaded the girl with Spanish waltzes on his guitar, the girl admired his impressive, handsome horse.

"I like this animal," the girl said with a sigh. She stroked Gypsy's mane timidly.

"I can take you for a ride," José said. They rode together bareback, and José told her to hug his waist. They trotted through the village as the entire tribe watched. Bridget bounced, nearly falling off.

"Hug me tighter," José told her. Her body cupped his and as Gypsy slowed to a walk, José knew he was in love with the girl and the girl knew she was in love with the horse.

The two engaged in a brief courtship; most of the time they rode Gypsy around the small area of the village, going in circles and kicking up black dust while everyone watched. This confused Bridget's mild mannered fiancé, who also happened to be her first cousin, but her father decided it was better business to marry her off to the *gringo*, with the hopes that a great fortune would spring out of this union with the white man.

Elsa could imagine him rafting down the Santos River, proud like an Indian, or sitting on his honey mare, Gypsy, while serenading his young bride as she looked down from her hut on stilts. She could see him roaming the land in search of his fortune with a treasure map in hand, however elusive it would remain.

Then Elsa began to have a recurring dream. She was in a raft floating down the gentle currents of a muddy, chocolate river. José was guiding her down the winding river in the creaking, old boat, with a wall of dense rainforest surrounding them, and mist rose like a blanket of cloudy smoke. The air was humid and so heavy it was hard to breathe and felt engulfing.

The buzzing and chirping of fauna rang in her ears, whereas the ripples of water hitting the sides of the craft murmured as soft as wind rustling leaves. A water snake stuck its large head out of the river and swam towards them. Then it slithered, long and wet, onto the raft and lifted its trunk at her feet.

Suddenly, it was no longer a snake but had transformed into Bridget. She was naked and sleek, her long black hair wrapped around her, hugging her body like a robe. Her face still resembled a snake more than a human but she smiled; Elsa was not frightened. Her eyes were black slits, and Elsa shied away from her otherworldly gaze. Bridget was holding an immense papaya, which she handed to Elsa.

She would hold the papaya cradled in her arms, and after a few moments, she would look down to see that it was a baby. Then she would wake up crying.

Chapter 11

Elsa's trauma of the robbery left her feeling cutoff from the rest of the world. She felt disconnected from any kind of normality and that left her unbearably alone. She was afraid to tell her parents. She knew her father would be angry and her mother distraught with the news. Elsa also knew that eventually she would have to tell them; it was a secret she just couldn't keep and almost three weeks had passed since the incident.

Even though she tried to focus on helping Margot, she still felt stuck in a separate reality that she believed no one could truly understand. She berated herself for being self-centered given her best friend's ordeal. But she just couldn't pull herself out of the deep quagmire of fear and despair.

Thoughts of Gustavo came, but they were too painful to entertain. They had spoken a few times and Gustavo always asked about her return to Peru, but she didn't tell him about the robbery. She couldn't bring herself to commit to a return date. And anyway, Margot still needed her. Their conversations always left Elsa melancholic. So she began to push him away from her mind, from her heart.

It was late in the afternoon and quiet. Elsa was in the living room; the blinds were closed, making the cabin dim and gloomy. She sat under the single lit lamp, trying to read a book written by an author she'd never heard of, set in some city in India she knew nothing about, and she reread the same page over and over, unable to make sense of anything.

She lifted her eyes from the book and scanned the room. The décor hadn't changed since she married Charles: the green upholstered couch looked worn-out and wilted; there were the same assemble-your-own bookcases and entertainment center that had always been there. It was a comfortable, cozy room yet it had become shabby.

Elsa didn't like to think about that, but now, looking around the living room and noticing the neglected piano sitting along a shadowed wall, made her think about the passing years. The grandfather clock stood in a dark corner, and the beating tick-tock began to grow louder and thunder in her ears as she became acutely aware of the inescapable passage of time.

She reached for the phone to call her parents to tell them that she loved them, and to tell them the truth about the events on the bus. She even decided to tell Gustavo about it by email. She didn't want to stay alone, be an island, forever. Her heart fluttered with the desire to live, to connect to her loved ones, and inside her chest it felt like the flapping of those desperate silk moths, so fragile yet eager to attract a mate before they fade away and die.

Miguel was furious with the news. He ranted, "I told you, but you didn't listen. I knew this would happen, the feeling was in my gut."

Miguel passed the phone to Josephine who cried and thanked God over and over for saving Elsa's life. Then her mother said, "Elsa why did you keep this from us? I can't believe you didn't tell us sooner."

"I just couldn't bear the thought. And I felt so guilty, like somehow it was my fault for not listening to dad." Elsa cried to her mom.

Elsa was hurt that her father blamed her for what happened, but she also knew that he was venting. She hoped that he would get over his anger and shower her with his affection after taking time to process what had happened.

Elsa then emailed Gustavo, telling him about the bus hijacking and her doubts about going back to Peru. Three days passed, and he still hadn't called her, so a nagging question began to torment her, am I destined be alone forever? It seemed that the more she pondered the question, the more she couldn't shake her insecurities.

Memories of making love to Gustavo stormed her brain. She pushed them away. Yet it was impossible, because the memories of him felt like something meaningful, a relationship that could have been real. She remembered his fingertip tracing her contours, his mouth on her body, and the delicious ache she had felt. She thought about his gentle ways, the smile that had eased her fears. He made her feel safe and loved in the short amount of time they shared together.

If she had any idea that things would turn out like this, with her in the states and too afraid to travel back to Peru, she would have savored it even more. She would have cherished each and every embrace, caress and kiss as if it were her last.

Elsa gazed out the window; nothing had changed, still gray and colorless, and she placed her hand on the pane, letting the coolness numb her fingers. And then she thought of "Storm Fear," which she had memorized in graduate school, and she whispered Frost's poem under her breath. *When the wind works against us in the dark…The beast, come out, come out.*

Her cell phone was ringing quietly in the background. Elsa made her way through the house, looking for the phone, but she didn't reach it in time. She saw that she had a missed call, but she didn't recognize the number. When she listened to the voicemail, she was completely taken aback to hear Charles's voice.

"Elsa, I heard from James about what happened in Peru. And I was calling to see if you're okay." Elsa remembered then that her brother's best friend was an old college friend of Charles. A strange coincidental web of connections, which now made Elsa realize that rumors were flying.

The message continued, "By the way, I'm not with Gillian anymore. Remember our spot? I still go every Monday night, if you want to meet me there. It would be great to see you, Elsa."

Elsa couldn't believe he was inviting her to Sam's Diner–or that he mentioned the girl who had broken up their marriage. She noticed the sadness in his voice, though Elsa didn't trust him.

What did he think would happen if they met at the diner? It was too late to rekindle anything–they were divorced. Elsa yelled into the dead phone, "What are you thinking, Charles? And you know what, you can drop that fake British accent, Chuck. You grew-up in the Valley, you pompous ass!" Elsa slammed the phone down on the table and broke into tears.

What would Angelica have done in this situation? Elsa imagined that Angelica never would have given up on life, even though she never again obtained romantic love after her husband died. She remember her grandmother's words to her: "Don't be afraid of love, it comes in all kinds of packages."

Her grandmother, Angelica, lived a full, happy life, even while remaining a grieving, faithful widow. And she was only thirty-two when Pablo Miguel died. Elsa believed she was more a saint than mortal. Angelica's faith was immaculate and sustaining, even to those who only experienced it vicariously in her presence.

By the end of her life, after so much loss, Angelica believed herself to be closer to the Virgin than most people. Angelica had a special, intimate relationship with Mary. The Virgin was not only a pious, omniscient figure but also Angelica's comrade. Their relationship was akin to friendship, a bond so great that Angelica could ask anything of Mary, and she would readily comply. If the day was sunny, it was a blessing bestowed by her. If Miguel's plane didn't crash getting to Peru, it was solely due to her will. If Angelica opened her eyes in the morning and was still alive, it was only because the Mother of God consented. But Angelica scolded her too, when things didn't go so well. It was a sisterhood, and her direct channel to reaching the heavens.

The next day, Margot sat at the kitchen table, helping to make dinner, chopping lettuce for a salad. She was regaining her strength daily. Elsa finished unloading the dishwasher, and cleared her throat. "I know you're going to be upset, Margot, but Charles called me yesterday. He had heard about the hijacking and wanted to check on me."

"My god. He's got some nerve. I hope you told him off." Margot was always tough when it came to Charles. The two had always clashed. Margot was fond of calling Charles a tight ass. After the divorce, Margot had tried to console Elsa by pointing out that she could never relate to a man who preferred cognac and Tchaikovsky over beer and Clapton.

Elsa decided not to mention the invitation to meet him at Sam's.

"What about Gustavo, Elsa? You've been strangely quiet on the subject." Margot stared at Elsa, waiting for her reply.

Elsa grabbed a rag and began wiping down the counters with forceful, exaggerated effort. Eventually she paused and turned to Margot. She let out a deep sigh and said, "We've talked a few times, but I just couldn't bring myself to tell him about what happened on the bus. I had the same feeling with my parents and Gustavo, like it was my fault somehow. And anyway, I wasn't sure about our future. Then I emailed him just a few days ago to tell him about the robbery, but he hasn't answered back." Elsa looked out the kitchen window with tears streaming down her face.

"I'm so sorry, honey. It was good that you finally told him. He'll answer back; he's probably without Internet. It seems like communication can be difficult from the mountains," Margot reassured Elsa.

Elsa knew she was right. Services could often be interrupted by any number of human and natural causes. There was no reason to believe he would intentionally avoid her.

Elsa wiped away her tears. She asked, "This may seem strange, but how would you feel about visiting a native healer?"

"You mean a shaman?" Margot put the chopped lettuce in a bowl.

Elsa sat down and rested her chin in her hands. "A co-worker at the university, actually she's one of the librarians, is Native American—Shawnee I believe. Her husband is a healer and she'd asked a few times if I would like to have a cleansing ceremony. It might be soothing."

"I don't know anything about it, what's involved?" Margot asked.

"It's simple really. I just thought it could symbolize a new beginning for us both."

"At this point, nothing could hurt." Margot shrugged and took a sip from her wine glass.

A couple of days later, Elsa and Margot were driving down a dirt road, which led to a small house obscured by an expansive front yard filled with pine trees. It was dusk, and the landscape was a still life of gray shadows, quiet and chilly. Billy Night Traveler came out of the house. He was tall and heavyset, with black hair flowing around his face. His face was soft and round, yet with deep creases around his eyes and across his forehead. He smiled, shook their hands, and led Elsa and Margot into the house.

Billy's wife, Rinay, offered them hot cider once they were all seated in the cozy living room. A fire was roaring in the fireplace and the smell of damp forest and smoke was comforting and reminded Elsa of her own cabin.

Billy said, "Elsa, I'll work on Margot first while you visit with Rinay in the other room. Are you wearing a bathing suit under those winter clothes, Margot?" Billy chuckled. He had explained that he would need their limbs bare to work the water on them. Although Margot initially protested to Elsa about stripping down, in the end she got over feeling self-conscious and agreed to wearing a tank top and panties.

After nearly an hour, Margot emerged looking relaxed and rosy skinned. "It's your turn, Elsa. You're going to love this."

Rinay offered Margot another cup of cider, and Elsa left to take her turn with the shaman.

Once settled on the soft couch, she relaxed. Billy tucked a light throw blanket over her, and they were ready to begin.

"Before we start I want to ask you something." Billy rubbed his hands together. His black hair flowed around his soft, kind face. "I see a lot of visitors around you—do you know them?"

"Visitors?" Elsa questioned.

"My ancestors are always around me, chanting and beating their drums. They come when I practice healing—sometimes even when I sleep," Billy explained.

He told her that he just accepted their presence as necessary and natural, as essential as his own breath. The elders still passed down their knowledge of healing and 'dream flight' to him, but it was his ancestors long gone by now who would catch him if he fell. His ancestors whispered to him through the forests and through the streams, arteries of the Klamath River.

They also whispered to the shaman as he practiced on his patients, people searching for remedies from any vast number of maladies of the body and spirit.

"Are they here to protect me?" Elsa asked.

"Your ancestors may protect you, but they also might need you to fulfill a task. Or perhaps they just like your company," he told Elsa.

Elsa closed her eyes. Now that Elsa knew that her great-grandfather was a murderer, would the spirits ever be at rest? Elsa hardly thought so. The ghosts had given no indication of giving up their benign haunting any time soon. She had already decided to tell her family the truth about the murder. She couldn't let the lie pass through generations any longer, especially for Nemesio and his family lineage.

Billy Night Traveler began to chant in the candlelit darkness while dipping his hands in warm water and massaging her bare limbs with his wet hands. He started with her legs, and he gently massaged each limb with the water. Elsa felt his soothing touch, firm yet also tender. As he wiped the water off her skin with his hands and massaged her, she felt like he was pulling off the weight she had been carrying: that unbearable weight of fear that had latched itself to her, the weight of trauma. He moved to her arms, and tugged and pulled at the limbs, so that the muscles stretched and relaxed. Again, she felt like years of tension were being pulled and tossed away. Then after a while, Elsa almost thought she heard his ancestors. As Billy sang, his voice began to reveal layers of tones and pitches, and Elsa was sure that there were many voices surrounding her. And as she listened to the array of visitors in that small room, tears ran down her face for the beauty of their melody, and the medicinal effect it had on her.

When Billy finished, he asked, "Something bad happened to you. I see the darkness trying to pull you in."

Elsa was taken aback, and she hesitated before answering. "Yes, there was an armed robbery."

Billy began to gather the bowls of water and fold the blanket on the couch. He blew out the lit candles, and clouds of smoke swirled.

"Did you forgive those young men?"

Elsa began to cry. She couldn't forgive them. She hated them.

"You know, there are many holy places with powerful spells, especially Peru. There's very special magic there. But sometimes there's ignorance and desperation, too. Some might call it evil. Either way, you need to forgive those boys," Billy said. Then he added, "I see an Indian near you, along with the line of your ancestors. He can teach you forgiveness."

Elsa thought about Nemesio.

Elsa and Margot left Billy's house and drove home along a winding, narrow road. Dust billowed in their wake.

"What did you think?" Margot asked as they turned into the driveway of the cabin.

"It was magical. I loved the feeling of the water and Billy's touch. Margot, something else happened. He told me that I could study the way of the shaman. I have the gift, he said." Elsa turned it over in her mind.

That night, gloominess overtook her. Yet Elsa decided to embrace the moment, and instead of anger she sought to forgive those desperate boys. She meditated on the face of the boy that held the gun to her. She imagined his face covered with a black scarf and those bulging red eyes with black centers, and then envisioned it surrounded by light. She meditated until she was able to transform it into a different face, a face without the mask and eyes softer, clearer and at peace.

Elsa used to have flying dreams once in a while–she was always on the beach. She was cautious at first, testing her lift-off by leaning into the wind, then gradually she'd ascend. It was the wind that carried her; she practiced using the gusts to rise and descend at will. She imagined that with practice she would gain the ability and confidence to lift even higher, but then she stopped having the dreams.

She remembered all of the plans she had made before boarding that bus, to make a home in Wayi, to fall in love again, to make a fresh start in life. She remembered the peace and calm she felt while watching the women weave, as she herself sat at the loom, a novice with Meli's hands helping to guide her with the picks. Those were times when all the worries of the world just evaporated, and she was wholly concentrated on the simple moment.

The dream returned and she began to soar. But now, rather than at the beach, she glided off Andean mountains and flew through valleys alongside condors. She visited Peru and conversed with Salvatore and Nemesio, she watched Gustavo as he helped his patients, and she observed the women sitting in a circle, weaving golden silk.

Then she watched as monstrous silk worms twirled themselves around and around weaving their own protective cocoon where they would hide and protect themselves while they metamorphosed into delicate moths. She watched this even as she slept soundly in her bed nestled in the redwood forest far, far away.

Chapter 12

The phone had been ringing faintly in the background. Elsa figured it was Margot; she couldn't fathom that Charles would call her again.

When she put the phone up to her ear, she could hear the deep, reassuring voice on the other end, "Elsa, are you there? It's me, Gustavo. Please tell me you're all right, please tell me." He pleaded.

Elsa couldn't speak at first; her chest was in a knot. She just couldn't catch her breath. The tears flowed, as she listened to Gustavo.

"Elsa, I was without Internet. I just read your email. Please, tell me you're okay."

"I wasn't hurt. I'm okay, but I really don't know about going back."

"I know it's been terrible, my sweet Elsa. Just as we were building something, I had to go away. I regret that now," Gustavo explained. "But it was an obligation, I had the trip planned months in advance."

"I know, I know." Elsa suddenly felt worried she sounded needy. The last thing she wanted was to come across as controlling or insecure.

"Honestly, I wish I hadn't gone away for so long. I wish I had stayed with you."

Elsa felt a wave of emotion rush through her body with his words. She felt the sincerity behind them. "I'm proud of you, Gustavo. And maybe I'll make it back to Peru someday."

"You promised me you were coming back. I'll go to California, and bring you back myself, if I have to," he said. "I'm not joking."

"I think I need just a little more time, but I want desperately to see you again." Elsa was sure about that.

"I will be waiting for you. Like I told you before. I promise you, Elsa."

When they ended the call, Elsa began to think about going back to Peru. She imagined resting in Gustavo's arms. But then her chest tightened and she held her breath. She could feel panic take over.

Elsa had been thinking more and more about Charles since his message. She still felt angry and hurt by his affair, but somehow she still couldn't move on. His invitation to meet him at Sam's lingered in the back of her mind. Sam's had been one of their regular hangouts and Elsa intentionally avoided the restaurant. But Monday evening, she found herself driving the winding road toward the coast.

Elsa entered the local diner, a place frequented by lumberjacks and fishermen. She glanced around the place, and it was nearly empty save for a few burly guys sitting at the counter. She sat at a corner table and ordered a slice of cherry pie and coffee. She sat alone, staring out the window and drinking the stale lukewarm coffee.

She wondered what she was really doing there. What did she hope to achieve? Maybe it was just curiosity, or some morbid sadistic need to test herself, or test Charles.

Sometime later, she heard the bell on the door of the restaurant ring and then recognized the voice calling out to the waitress. "I'll take the usual, Lori."

Charles sat down at a table, and ran his fingers through his tousled gray hair. Elsa scooted closer to the window at her table and slid a few inches down into the booth. She knew she'd regret being there. Now that he had actually shown up, she had no idea what to do.

She worked even harder to obscure herself in the large cushions of the booth. She used her hands to hide her face. Elsa peeked over at him. She watched Charles pull out a thick novel from his satchel.

Lori wandered over to Elsa and refilled her coffee. "It's a slow night," she said as she gave Elsa a wink and nodded toward Charles.

Charles was handsome in that intellectual kind of way. The way a teacher's good looks can't be separated from his air of smartness. He wore a tan corduroy blazer with blue jeans and black Converse sneakers, and his gray stubble only added to his rakish charm.

Elsa mustered up her courage, and finally said in a firm voice, "Hello, Charles. Funny running into you here."

He seemed genuinely surprised.

"Elsa, is that you?" He cleared his throat before adding, "I didn't expect you to come."

"It's pretty bad out there," Elsa said as she turned her head away from him. The rain beating against the windowpane seemed to be an invitation to bunker down in their cozy corner of the diner. Elsa watched the drops of water stick, and then roll across the glass, making squiggly designs like microorganisms in a petri dish. A flash of lightning illuminated the parking lot.

"Would you like to share dinner with me? Remember, the chicken fried steak is always enough for two," Charles said casually.

Charles rose from his table and slid into the booth with her. "You look great, Elsa."

"Thanks."

"I've actually starting writing my book, Elsa. All those ideas are finally getting onto paper." Charles had talked about writing a book for years, especially at parties and social functions where he had an audience to practice with.

Elsa now noticed his boyish expression beneath the cool façade, seeking her approval no doubt. Charles always needed validation.

"That's great. I'm sure it will be a huge success, Charles." She didn't mean to let sarcasm ruin the moment. Elsa was quickly reminded of the tenor of rivalry that shadowed their marriage. It was a lurking competitiveness, which neither would acknowledge until it was too late.

Soon Elsa found herself sharing a plate of chicken and mashed potatoes with Charles. Maybe it was the storm outside, an excuse not to drive the windy, dark roads. Maybe it was Lori, and her winks and nods and talk of slow nights. Maybe it was doubts about Gustavo and her desire to be sure once and for all.

Elsa sat and listened to Charles tell her all about his novel. It was a tale of adventure set in the Midwest during the Great Expansion of the 1800s. There were battles fought and hardships on the wagon trails, savagery and nobility, slavery and freedom, love and heartache–all of the drama of Manifest Destiny.

Elsa was surprised to find that the story aroused her. Charles was rather prosaic in his recounting of massacres, famines and gunfights. But as Elsa listened to Charles' slightly nervous summary, she imagined herself as an Indian guide, like Sacagawea. It was thoughts of Gustavo, and his body entwined with hers, that had her breathless. Gustavo's lips against her skin, his mouth on hers, his throbbing inside her, these sensations overtook her. Gustavo became Meriwether Lewis mounting her in a meadow of green with wild flowers blooming in abundance, and Charles had no idea as he ordered his last cup of coffee for the night.

The rain had lightened, and Elsa thought it was a good time to exit.

"Great to see you're doing well, Charles. Good luck with the novel," Elsa said as she pulled herself out of the booth. Her body seemed to have molded into the plastic cushion.

"Are you sure you want to leave alone?" Charles ran his fingers through his hair, and let his elbow rest on the counter. He tilted his head and grinned.

Did he really think Elsa would have a fling with him? Did he believe she could ever really forgive him? Forgiveness maybe with time, but she could never forget.

Elsa could think only of Gustavo.

"Yeah, I'm sure," she said.

Seeing his sudden disinterest as Charles gazed out the window, Elsa knew he hadn't expected her to accept his invitation. It was merely a ruse. They parted with a brief and cool pat on the shoulder.

She drove home along the winding, narrow road. At her cabin, Elsa climbed the wet steps leading to her deck and stood facing the redwood forest just beyond her doorstep. The night was cold and damp; she zipped up her fleece jacket.

Elsa realized that she had had a headache all day—a dull ache in the back of her head that went almost unnoticed, like an annoying sensory impression—a buzzing or a bright light.

Then in the dimness, Elsa caught sight of a large beetle as it crawled by her left foot. She watched as it scuttled around in circles, as if confused by the sudden abyss in its path. It had come across the edge of a plank of wood at the end of the deck. It could have made a turn to the right or left, but Elsa saw that it wanted to move straight ahead, even its tiny head looked over the edge as if contemplating jumping. Elsa knew exactly how it felt, and so she lifted it gently into her hand and carried it to the entrance of the sweet, rain scented forest.

"Find your way," she said. She watched as the green iridescent bug scurried over rocks and organic debris.

"Margot, I've decided to go back to Peru." Elsa had been back home for nearly two months.

Elsa and Margot were sitting at a small table in Margot's bookstore. Margot had finished her radiation treatments, and she was surprisingly resilient and in good spirits.

"Are you sure you're ready?" Margot closed the open account book resting on the table. She placed her arms on the table and rested her chin in her hands. Margot glanced around the small store and sighed. "Did I thank you enough for all your help, Elsa? I couldn't have done this without you, you know that."

"Yes, you've thanked me plenty. Now that you're recovering, why don't you come with me, Margot? I'd love to show you Peru, with all its beauty and wonder. It would be a nice break after everything you've been through. What do you say?" Elsa brightened with the prospect.

"Well, I wouldn't mind seeing this place you can't seem to live without—you'd think the house was George Clooney for Christ's sake! And Gustavo, well there's just no words." Then she added more thoughtfully, "The truth is I don't think I'm up for it quite yet. Let's plan for it down the road."

Elsa recalled Margot's trips to Thailand and New Zealand. Margot had always been adventurous. Now Elsa realized how her illness had taken its toll on Margot. "Yes, let's plan for it soon then."

"What about California, Elsa? You won't miss it?" Margot asked softly.

Elsa thought about her cabin and the old growth redwoods in her backyard forest. She felt a tug at her chest, a pang of regret. "So many memories," she sighed. "I wanted a fresh start, but I felt stuck until I went to Peru. Yes, I'll miss California but I need change even more."

California felt like a lost love as much as Charles did. It would always be there though, and when she closed her eyes she could feel the wind trying to lift her from the cliffs along the rocky seashores. She could smell the damp mulch of the forest floor and hear the creeks and feel the smooth coldness of the stones from the fresh water against her skin. But, she knew it was time to move on.

"I'm going to miss you, my sweet friend." Margot leaned over and hugged Elsa.

Chapter 13

Angelica had been sent to boarding school in Cuzco, where all the other European immigrants scattered throughout the Andes sent their daughters for an upright and proper Catholic education. To come home for holidays, she traveled by train and then rode in a horse-drawn buggy to the Acutambo Valley. It was on one of these routine visits home that her party crossed paths with an impressive military convoy.

The soldiers had set up a check post at a long, precariously hanging bridge. The narrow suspension bridge dangled across the canyon, high above the raging Apurimac River, providing a perfect blockade: there was only one way across. There they had captured several suspected insurgents and other assorted criminals. They marched them down the rocky cliff to the riverbed, making them carry rocks and boulders to place underneath the road, to fortify the retaining wall in preparation for the rainy season. At night, the prisoners were rounded up and made to sleep in the middle of the bridge while soldiers stood guard at both ends.

The captain explained to Angelica, "*Señorita*, I'm sorry to detain you, but we are on the lookout for rebels and bandits. It's really for your own protection."

"My own protection, *Señor?* I could show you a thing or two in these mountains! I know these rebels, for we've grown up together, sprouted from the very same minerals of the earth."

"Anyway, we must detain you a while longer to assure your safety," he said.

Angelica readily recognized Nemesio among the group behind him.

"And what of that young man there," Angelica replied, pointing towards the disheveled Indian who was sliding along the dirt trail, billowing dust as he trudged a large rock from the river.

He kept his head down while passing the rock to another. Then he walked back down to the river, trudging slowly and hunched over.

"That, *Señorita*, is a true outlaw. That bastard was caught leading a posse about to torch a hacienda just twenty kilometers from here." Angelica stood silent.

Nemesio lifted his head and looked up toward the ridge where Angelica stood. For a moment, they were both still. Nemesio was surprised, but then he felt a surge of something darker.

Just then a ruckus broke out and loud shouts were heard. Nemesio ran along the river, splashing and stumbling as he tried to bolt away. The soldiers immediately pulled their rifles and waited just a brief instant before firing in unison at the fugitive. He ran a few more yards, unsteady and lurching, before making a splash into the water. He then lay motionless, face down in the shallow waters of the riverbank.

For a brief instant as he lay in the water, Nemesio remembered how, as a boy, he had run out of his adobe home, down the narrow dirt road and into the center of town. It was the most anticipated day of the year, and his heart had pounded in his small chest as he neared the plaza. He worked his way through the crowd, searching for the bull.

Upon reaching the gate of the stall, Nemesio held his breath in awe. The stall was as big as the bull, encasing the animal in a cage of steel. The men, reeking of alcohol, tied the bull to the steel rods with thick rope, and Nemesio watched the beast snort defiantly. It was drenched in sweat, making its black coat shimmer over the taut muscles of its torso, bursting into mountains of bulges and swells. Nemesio leaned in closer and felt the bull's hot, moist breath. At least it was cool in the Andes, and the altitude kept the air from stagnating into a suffocating heat.

The scene was dizzying as crowds, drunk from barrels of chicha–fermented fruit and corn–yelled and cheered sending the animal into a fit of desperation. Nemesio looked around and everything seemed intensified. There were colorful banners and decorations throughout the plaza. All of the people wore dazzling colors, hats adorned with lace and ribbons, and masks of papier-mâché resembling creatures of pagan origins. Catholic crosses, images of saints and candles amassed into huge altars carried down the street in procession.

The crowd continued to gather in the plaza: children, elders, mothers and fathers, families celebrating the annual Yawar Fiesta. Chickens, goats, and mangy dogs ran loose, adding more mayhem to the occasion. Suddenly the crowd hushed at the sight of several men carrying an immensely large bird. The sight of this other beast, just as majestic and impressive as the bull, being ceremoniously carried into the plaza, held the entire town in suspense. The condor wasn't domesticated like the bull, but rather had been caught in a trap, lured by the carrion of sheep on a mountainside.

The next hour seemed like an eternity to Nemesio, and perhaps also to those two sudden adversaries: two animals that normally would have ignored each other, for under different circumstances their worlds would never collide. That is, unless the bull happened to take a fall over a mountain trail to end up a carcass for the scavenger to feast upon.

The beasts were armed for the duel. First, there was the gruesome undertaking of stabbing the bull with a sharp, pointed spear. Men dug deep into its flesh, making holes where two thick steel rings were jabbed through the meaty part of the back, below the neck and over the shoulder blades where the muscle protrudes like a knoll. Once the rings were clamped on securely the men embraced one another and passed around a bottle, taking swigs of a syrupy moonshine. Nemesio saw that the bull was frantic but immobilized; blood trickled down its shoulders and out of its nose, mixing the color of torture to the moist heat of its breath.

The next step required the pre-selected, most worthy men, which included Nemesio's father, to lift the monstrous vulture and carry it toward the stall. The crowd was completely silent, and yet faintly, in the background, the whispers of prayers could be heard. The prayers, in Quechua, were a blend of Catholic verses and pre-Spanish ancient hymns of a mysterious religion—a religion honoring the Apus Mountain gods and the condor now being hoisted onto the back of the bull. There was no graceful, easy way to accomplish this, but in a frantic blur of commotion and uproar, and within a furious instant, the condor's talons were tightly wound with ropes to the steel rings attached to the bull's back.

Now there was no time to waste, and led on by the crowd's cheers and taunts in chorus, the bull was set loose with the condor fastened to its back. The villagers watched with wonder the duel between the two animals: one of Spanish origin, and of course, the other, the great condor, as native and authentic to Peru as the Incas themselves. The condor won the battle; the condor always won.

The condor pecked out the bull's eyes first, and then tore into the flesh relentlessly with its sharp, carnivorous beak. The bull was left defenseless, save for throwing itself around haphazardly, running and bucking, but without much force. The bull was blinded, and then chopped into mincemeat alive, and all to riotous shouts and cries.

Each year Nemesio witnessed the event, and as he grew up he began to understand the bull. *It was Spanish: conquistador, ruler of men, and a tyrant. It was the seeker of gold, looter of riches, and yet it was all they had become and its blood ran through their veins.* Nemesio loved the bull and despised him too, and in the end the condor always won, during the Yawar Fiesta.

As he lay dying, Nemesio remembered that the condor was set free to fly away from the blood and violence in the center of town. The bird soared up into the serene caves of the rocky mountainsides where an ancient civilization once resided and now stood in ruins. When taking flight it was always majestic and extraordinary, taking Nemesio's breath away.

Elsa walked to the main plaza. She relished the familiarity of Cuzco as she moseyed along the cobblestone streets. Elsa recognized the same silvery shimmer, sunlight flickering over gray stones across the city. The sky was royal blue; the sun was obscured by the surrounding hillsides and shadows, which diffused over the plaza. A layer of dew covered the city and the air was brisk; the altitude made Elsa feel lightheaded. It was chilly yet invigorating.

The streets around the plaza had been closed off and people lined the sidewalks and crowded the balconies overlooking the plaza. Elsa worked her way through, and it wasn't overly crowded, just a mingling kind of crowd: a few tourists with cameras dangling from their necks, shopkeepers, children and old people.

From a distance Elsa could see the large mass of people swaying down the street toward her. It was an amazing sight: the ten-foot Jesus on a crucifix being lifted and carried by a dozen men leading the procession. The dark Jesus was draped with purple, red and gold fabric and a sarong was tied around his waist. He was strewn with garlands of red flowers.

Elsa had always heard about *El Señor de los Temblores*, but she never thought she'd see him. The Lord of Earthquakes was the patron saint of Cuzco. The procession was rare to witness because they never set an exact date. Elsa was watching the procession get closer; the tall crucifix pulsated to the rhythm of the single moving body of worshippers and swung to and fro. From the silver base, smoke billowed from the incense and candles amassed at his feet.

Elsa had to look up to take in the massive figure as it passed by. All the while, the people on the balconies threw red flower petals by the handfuls down upon the Jesus. The petals scattered the streets and floated down, carried across the plaza; the crimson silky petals stuck to everything. Elsa had petals in her hair, on her clothes, even down her blouse. The scent of incense lingered in the air.

As Elsa watched *El Señor* pass by, she inhaled the smoky, sweet incense and let the taste of it settle in the back of her throat. She let a rain of flower petals fall onto her while saying prayers. She didn't want to be selfish, she thought about peace in the Middle East, the hungry and miserable living in squalor in the shantytowns of Lima and all around the globe. She thought about people with cancer and mothers with dead children and all of the misery of the world, but she couldn't help her own prayers that came spewing out, up toward the black Jesus swaying on the cross wearing a sarong and flower leis. He seemed like a Jesus for everyone—this island paradise Jesus in the middle of the cold Andes.

She prayed, please help me find peace. "I'm not dead after all," she muttered.

She wondered about Gustavo and how it would be when they finally saw each other in person. They had been talking on the phone and emailing frequently over the past weeks, and he always encouraged her to come back. He was loving and supportive over the phone.

The street sweepers dressed in baby-blue jumpers and carrying large bulky straw brooms began to sweep away the flower petals into large piles on the street corners.

Elsa walked to meet Paco, and begin her journey to Wayi. When Paco saw her, he said, "This town ain't big enough for the two of us." He chuckled and winked at her. They embraced, and Elsa climbed into the battered, dusty Toyota.

This time, she and Paco made no tourist stops. Elsa wanted to make a straight shot to Wayi. Elsa recognized the same section of road where she and Paco had encountered the roadblock. She remembered the fear of facing the men in uniforms, carrying machine guns, and how Paco was able to turn the situation around.

Elsa couldn't help feeling anxiety now; her palms were sweating and she felt a knot in her stomach. She told herself, just stay calm. Nothing bad can happen, you've already been through the worst. She forced her thoughts away from the bus hijacking, and instead focused on the house. She thought about Gustavo, although that gave her some anxiety, as well.

They began to enter into the area with a familiar scent of anise, and Paco pointed out vicuña on the hillsides. Elsa waved at children standing on the side of the road. Paco honked at the cows, as they lazily crossed.

When they finally pulled up to the house, Paco wore a grin that gathered and crinkled his whole face. Elsa saw the Gomez Family standing on the porch and she opened the car door and jumped out.

Paco began unloading luggage from the trunk. But the kids, barefoot and happy, were already racing across the yard to greet her. Elsa hugged the children to her chest, telling them, "I missed you all so much. I brought you presents, just like I promised." The children cheered and laughed. Elsa looked forward to seeing their faces when they received the new clothes and toys.

Paco called the children over to him. He gave each of the children high-fives and passed out Hershey bars.

When Elsa glanced up, she saw Gustavo come out the front door of the house. He walked to the edge of the porch, leaned into the railing, and looked eagerly toward the car.

Elsa felt a tightening in her gut, and the mixed emotions of ecstasy and nervous uncertainty kept her still and breathless. She slapped her cheeks with the palms of her hands and blew out long and hard. Tears were already running from the corners of her eyes. Elsa stood for a moment, unable to move toward the house. Yet she and Gustavo had already locked eyes, and both were taking in the moment slowly.

Elsa wondered why she couldn't be braver, why everything had to be so damn hard. She gave herself a quick mental pep talk. She walked slowly up the pathway, with her head held high, watching Gustavo's expression as she neared him.

His smile was the same relaxed, easy grin she had remembered. His eyes were soft and kind.

As she got closer, Gustavo moved to greet her. She fell into his arms and buried her head into his chest as he whispered in her ear, "You are more beautiful than I even remembered, my beloved Elsa. I missed you so much. I don't ever want to lose you again."

With those words, Elsa felt the tight knots in her chest unwind. She felt light and free as her fears unclenched and fluttered away like moths on a breeze.

That night, after a family dinner on the patio with the Gomez family, Elsa took out the presents she brought. While the family delighted in opening packages, Elsa could feel Gustavo's eyes on her. Every time she looked at him, it was as if a wave of warm energy connected them. She felt distracted and flushed.

"Meli, I thought you would like these." Elsa handed over a pair of new sneakers, as well as pretty leather sandals with a short heal. Meli beamed as she tried them on.

Hernán was already playing with the Swiss Army knife. The children, one by one, gave Elsa a hug as they headed off to bed.

"*Gracias, Señora Elsa,*" Meli said as she gave Elsa one more hug. "You are so kind and generous to bring us these gifts. We missed you while you were gone, and now we are so happy for your return." Elsa smiled and took in a deep breath. She once again felt the pull and heat of Gustavo's presence as he sat across the table and watched the festive occasion.

Gradually everything quieted down, and Elsa and Gustavo were alone on the patio. She walked over and held her hand out to him. He smiled and took her hand, as she led him up the staircase to the master bedroom, where they had spent so many blissful nights making love, and neither spoke a word.

This time, rather than hesitant and timid, Elsa was eager and burning with passion. She had spent so many nights alone in California, dreaming of Gustavo, imagining this moment. Upon entering the room, she embraced him, letting her hands run over his body as they kissed deep on the mouth. Gustavo cupped her breast with one hand, while the other hand fondled her. Elsa moaned with desire.

They could barely remove their clothes by the time Gustavo entered her hard and deep. They both paused and looked into each other's eyes. He whispered, "My god, Elsa. You make me feel whole. I love you." And then he began to move slow and rhythmically until Elsa cried out in ecstasy.

Afterward, as they lay on the bed out of breath and moist with perspiration, Elsa asked, "Did you mean what you said, Gustavo? Or was it the heat of the moment?"

Gustavo took her hand and kissed it. He replied, "Yes, I meant it. I love you, Elsa."

Elsa sighed deeply and said, "I love you, too." She snuggled into his side and closed her eyes.

The next day, Elsa pulled up weeds and picked fruits. It felt good to work. She sat once again with Meli at the loom, learning all over how to maneuver the picks. Even though it was slow, and she wasn't very good at it, the weaving felt like a sort of meditation, calming her. She hoped to improve with practice. Then, Elsa helped clean and prepare lunch in the kitchen alongside Meli. Elsa was reminded of the inconvenience of no running hot water, but rationing wouldn't be a problem now that they entered the rainy season.

The stream that wound its way through the outskirts of the property was no longer a trickling brook, but had become a muddy, flowing cascade of water. Elsa was reminded of the odd folktale that Paco had relayed to her on their first journey through the Andes, and she knew that mudslides became a real concern during this time of year. Meli told her that they had already lost a goat to the rapids of the creek.

Elsa set up the magnificent upstairs bedroom once again with her things, ready to confront any ghostly appearances. She was determined to keep the master bedroom for herself, and for Gustavo when he would spend the night with her.

That evening, Elsa and Gustavo stood together on the porch. Elsa asked Gustavo, "Will you be staying over tonight?"

"I need to be at the clinic early. I'm getting a visit from some of the Abancay hospital staff tomorrow."

"Tomorrow night then?" she asked.

Gustavo leaned in and kissed Elsa softly on the mouth and squeezed her hand. His kiss turned hard and passionate. Elsa felt heat rise in her body and an ache of desire swell in her groin.

When Gustavo left, Elsa went to her bedroom feeling slightly delirious and breathless. She lay on the bed, staring at the ceiling, imagining Gustavo's return the following night. She gradually drifted off to sleep.

Elsa awoke, sometime in the middle of the night, with the strange sensation of someone standing over her, watching her. There was no one, though she did see a shadow move across the white wall, the same shadow she had seen so many other nights during her previous stay in the country house. She heard the gentle pacing on the wood floor, and looked across the room, where she expected to see her grandfather, Salvatore. She was surprised to see Nemesio, walking slowly across the room with his head down, wearing his colorful woolen *chullo,* and barefoot. Elsa sat up and watched him.

Nemesio slowly approached her, and then he stood still just a few feet away, with his head bowed. Elsa heard him whisper in Quechua. She thought about the stories she had heard from Hernán, as he spoke about the injustices that his grandfather had endured–being assaulted by the Plague and then accused of a crime he didn't commit, running away and remaining a fugitive in the mountains.

"I'm sorry, Nemesio. I'm sorry for the way my family treated you." Elsa spoke out to the apparition with some fear, but also with conviction. She began to cry. He took a step closer, and Elsa reached out to him and took his hand. She felt the hand solid and real in her own. It was flesh and bone. Then when she looked into Nemesio's face, it wasn't his face at all. It was Meli standing by the bed, holding Elsa's hand.

"Meli, is that you?" Elsa asked, suddenly confused. Elsa shook herself awake.

"*Sí, Mamá*, I came to check on you and heard you talking to someone."

"Did you see him, Meli? Did you see Nemesio?" Elsa asked, nearly pleading to Meli for reassurance.

"I thought I heard someone speaking, and that's why I came into the room. But I didn't see anyone, *Mamá*," Meli said, as she gently helped Elsa lie back down, tucking the blankets around her.

As Elsa drifted off to sleep once again, she thought about Nemesio and the feeling of his hand in hers. Then Elsa realized that Meli called her *Mamá*. She smiled to herself and felt a deep sense of relief. The subtle switch from the title *Doña* to *Mamá* was a sign of endearment from Meli. Elsa hoped this meant a closer relationship between them.

Chapter 14

A couple of days after the ghostly visit by Nemesio, Meli told Elsa, "I'm going away for a few days. I'll be back before Sunday." She had already taken her children to her mother's house.

Elsa asked, "Is everything all right, Meli?"

Meli explained to Elsa, "It's all gone on long enough. I think I should have done something sooner." Elsa felt a change in Meli; she had begun to soften.

Meli explained to Elsa her plan to travel into the Amazon. Meli would have to hike the trails alone, with a mule as her sole companion, down the eastern slope of the Andes Mountains until she reached the lush blanket of the jungle and entered into the Department of Loreto, and the small town of Porras, too small to appear on any map. Here was the heartland of the curanderos. Shamans and medicine men abounded and it was the rainforest's industry, just in the same way that the highest Andes bred weavers, or the sea bred fishermen, Loreto bred curanderos: witchdoctors with enigmatic and supernatural powers.

After she left, Hernán told Elsa not to worry. His wife had her own mysterious ways.

Five days later, an elder from Porras accompanied Meli back home, and his arrival created quite a stir. Elsa was surprised to find the man sleeping on the back porch early one morning, but by midday his arrival had attracted all the villagers to their front yard. People gathered carrying white candles, and altars of saints, and some took advantage and sold grilled hot dogs or corn on the cob to the crowd. Children played soccer and elders chanted.

The curandero was impressive looking, with his long shiny black hair, intricately woven dress and feet encrusted with the salts of the earth. He smelled of damp forest and his figure gave way to the semblance of fluttering wings and shimmering light with pockets of deep, dark shadows.

He wandered through the yards and in the house, chanting and praying, carrying lit smudge sticks and a wooden cross decorated with grotesque, strange figures; a talisman with a mélange of Christian and pagan adornments. A small bottle of holy water, painted clay figurines, dried herbs, an image of the Virgin, a condor feather, and *Lucíary* beads made of dried seeds and goat hooves were all attached to the cross by course twine. At night, he kneeled by a campfire lit in the backyard, drinking from a ceramic cup, occasionally throwing up into a bucket. Elsa could hear him retching from inside the house.

After his second day of sitting at the fire, strolling throughout the grounds, and chanting, he now stood in the center of the front yard, surrounded by the congregation of villagers. Elsa was the most intrigued of the onlookers. The shaman stood still and ceremoniously proclaimed, "There has been great evil in this place. One evil was eliminated by the evil act of another, however two evils can never make a blessing. Now both evils have been carried away down the creek to be cleansed and emptied into the great river. So be it."

That was all he said: no grand prophecies, nor explanations, just a declaration for peace and tranquility to be restored. Elsa felt at peace with his short statement. She thought about the goodness of life and new beginnings. She knew that the secret of her great-grandfather's crime would be revealed. Although it would bring pain and grief to her father, and to Aunt Lina, she hoped it would help set right the injustice to Nemesio's family. She also hoped that the shaman's declaration was indeed a fact, and that Aunt Esther, Nemesio, and Salvatore were finally at rest.

After the shaman left, the master bedroom felt different. It still felt alive, the way doors swung open, the floors creaked and the walls sighed—but not like a haunted room anymore, more like a tired room that had seen a lot in its day. It seemed to sigh and tilt from time to time. Or, that was the way Elsa liked to see things.

To Elsa, everything had a life of its own, a history and a story to tell. Elsa felt the presence of Lucía and Angelica in the spacious room–amongst the wood beams, rustic furnishings, and vases of flowers.

She adorned the room with the golden silk woven by Meli, some dyed deep reds, purples, and blues. The curtains, doilies on the nightstand, the throw blanket over the bed were all woven from those tenacious silkworms living, mating, weaving, metamorphosing, perishing in the shed out back. In a strange way, Elsa missed Salvatore and Nemesio and felt sorry that they seemed to have moved on. Then Elsa realized that she herself was ready to move on and leave the past behind.

It was nearing mid-December and Elsa was anxious to have everything ready in time for Christmas. There was a lot to get done. The rooms had to be cleaned, there was shopping to do, food to stock up; the turkey was set loose in the backyard to fatten. The children chased it around, until Meli would make them stop, saying, "*Dejan el pavo.* You're going to make the meat tough."

A week later, Paco's beat-up Toyota came down the road spewing dust and gray smoke—crowded with people. As soon as he pulled up, Miguel, Josephine, and Lina climbed out with bags and limbs unfolding, tumbling out of the cramped space. Josephine helped Paco unload the car.

Elsa watched her father, as he stood firm, facing the country house with his arms resting across his chest. Elsa wondered what he was thinking. It had been so many years since her father had been there, visiting with his brother to discover a small portion of the family's dark past.

Aunt Lina stood next to Miguel and put her arm around him. She tilted her head, as if contemplating those mysteries that were buried and forgotten so long ago. Elsa walked from the porch and down the walkway toward the car.

"The house looks exactly the same. The bougainvillea is the same color purple that I always remembered," Lina said to her brother.

Elsa looked at the bright vines draped over the front of the house. The sunflowers were in bloom across the yard. She felt proud of the house.

Elsa approached and Miguel hugged his daughter. "I can't believe I'm back here after all these years. Lucía never told us the truth, but I'm glad to know. It's no wonder the house was haunted."

"Don't worry, *Papá.* The ghosts told me they won't come after you."

"Ay, silly girl. Now you're pulling my leg," Miguel said as they all walked up to the house together arm in arm.

"You are joking, aren't you?" Lina asked.

Elsa laughed. "We'll have to wait and see."

Miguel only shook his head. He added, "You know your brother wanted to come, but he couldn't leave his wife and kids, you know how it is."

"Sure, Dad. Don't worry." She squeezed her father's hands. Elsa was just relieved that Alejandro agreed not to sell the house. Elsa was able to convince him that it made a good long-term investment, as she explained that the value of properties in Peru would only continue to rise with the growing economy.

Elsa embraced Josephine at the door. "Mom, I'm so happy that you're here."

It was overwhelming. It had been several months since they had all been together, and now here it was, Christmas. There was nonstop commotion in the days that followed as the women baked, glazed, broiled and boiled everything from sweet potatoes, common in Peruvian cuisine, to cranberries, impossible to find in Peru but which Josephine had brought in cans. The turkey out back was another matter.

"My God! Please, don't tell me that they're going to ring that bird's neck." Josephine said with her nose scrunched up.

"I have to admit, it's one big bird. I don't see how we can manage it," Miguel said as they all sat in the back porch. They watched the turkey as it pecked around the grass, making gurgling sounds.

"It's a rather ugly creature," Lina added.

"*Bueno*, here's what we will have to do." Hernán began to explain with an authoritative tone, and he actually knew what to do by the sound of it. "We have to get the bird drunk first. Don Miguel can hold the bird down while I pour pisco into its mouth. Then we wait until the bird stumbles, wobbles and then keels over. That's the way you kill a turkey."

Everyone stared at him with jaws hung open. They thought he was joking until he said, "Not only is it the easiest way, but the pisco will make the meat tender."

"I hate to say it, but he's right." Miguel said. He had seen it done before. The ladies went inside to avoid the spectacle.

It was Christmas Eve, and as the evening approached, the last of the guests arrived. Elsa became impatient, and went to the front door every few minutes, looking out the window eagerly. She couldn't wait for her parents to meet Gustavo. She was sure that they would love him. She nearly bounced up and down when Gustavo's Cherokee Jeep pulled up to the front of the house. He had been away a few days, again working with the same organization to vaccinate children, this time in a remote area of the mountains. Gustavo made sure to not leave for overly long stretches, and Elsa had gotten used to his brief absences.

She even accompanied him on one trip for a few days. They drove along a dirt road following the Apurimac River, and once they reached a dead end, the small team trekked half a day to an outpost in the high mountains. There the Indians congregated for check-ups and medical treatment. Women trekked for hours, many carrying small children in papooses of brilliant colors. The children were rosy cheeked, but the altitude left dry cracks over their skin, and they all had runny noses. The diet of plenty of *cancha*–crunchy corn kernels–and very few sweets, kept their teeth strong and healthy. Only one child arrived with an intestinal bug that left him feverish and lethargic, and the mother told Gustavo that her son had had diarrhea for weeks. The team was able to give her antibiotics for the little boy. Elsa enjoyed helping, and she felt that it was something she could do more often.

Now Gustavo stood at the door wearing jeans and a wool blazer and holding a bouquet of wildflowers. Elsa opened the door beaming and he leaned in for a long, slow kiss.

"These are for you, my love. But now these poor flowers look so colorless and dull compared to you."

Elsa was flushed and glowing as she called to Miguel. "*Papá*, come here. I want you to meet my friend, Gustavo." Elsa winked at Gustavo, as her father joined them. They shook hands and patted each other firmly on their backs.

Elsa could tell that Gustavo was pleased. He tilted his head and smiled, his dark-green eyes reflecting light. He told her father, "Don Miguel, your daughter is in good hands."

"She tells me you're a doctor," Miguel said.

"Yes, I did my residency in Boston. So many of my countrymen leave once they are professionals, yet I felt a duty to come back and start my practice here at home." There was a pause, and then Gustavo added, "I love your daughter, Don Miguel."

Elsa blushed and squeezed Gustavo's hand. Miguel studied the two for a moment, before patting Gustavo on the back firmly once again. "Yes, I can see that. I'm glad to know she's happy."

Miguel and Gustavo chatted, while Josephine began to gather everyone to the table for dinner. They had pushed two long tables together, one they had to borrow from a restaurant in town. Elsa used the tablecloths made from the silk. Large vases overflowed with sunflowers, candles were lit, bowls and dishes started to fill the table and the children ran around and around, laughing and playing. Everything is just as it should be, thought Elsa.

Elsa paused for a moment and took in a breath. She felt a calm settle in her core, and it was so profound, so deep, that she couldn't move or speak for a moment. She glanced around the table, and slowly took in the faces of her loved ones. Her parents were side by side, just like they had been always, supporting each other, leaning on each other, through life. Aunt Lina was strong and proud, and independent. Gustavo beamed at Elsa, smiling in that way that reassured her. With Meli and Hernán, she had had to work to build their relationship, and she appreciated gaining their trust over time and with effort.

There was collective goodwill as everyone sat around the table. Elsa wiped a tear from her eye, and said, "*Papá,* would you please say the grace."

When Elsa sat down, Gustavo took her hand and kissed it. He leaned in and whispered in her ear, "I love you, Elsa. More than you will ever know."

They all ate, and laughed and told stories well into the night, until the kids fell asleep on the couch, the wine was gone and the drunken turkey was just bones on a platter. And once it had quieted down, the kitchen was clean and people were nodding off from over-eating, Elsa went to the front porch and sat on the bench to watch stray animals and the occasional villager stroll by. She gazed at the stars and the mountains; one white peak glowed in the distance. Josephine joined her daughter.

"Gustavo is very charming, Elsa. I see that look in his eye, he adores you." Josephine gently pulled a lock of Elsa's hair.

"I didn't want to jinx it. I still have to take everything a day at a time." Elsa could hear him talking to Miguel and Hernán through the open window. Their voices were muffled, but his slight accent was rich and distinct.

"I half expect a covered wagon to lumber by out here," Josephine said. "It's so peaceful."

"There's a shooting star." Elsa pointed. "The constellations are so different in the southern hemisphere. This sky is amazing; it seems like many more stars than in the north." The two sat in silence for a few moments, admiring the bright, crowded star-filled sky.

"You're staying." Josephine stated this as if making a declaration, maybe for her own acceptance.

"Yes, I'm staying." Elsa repeated. She hugged her mom, and Josephine took her daughter's hand.

"I don't blame you. Peru lured me in once, a long time ago." Josephine sighed, and then she rose, saying, "I should check on Meli. She might need a hand."

Just as Josephine went inside, Gustavo came out carrying a glass of wine. "A sip?" He held the glass out to Elsa. And as she sipped, he buried his face in her neck and nibbled her earlobe. Just then, Hernán appeared in the doorway and asked apologetically, "Señor Gustavo, I'm sorry to interrupt, but if you can come with me, I need a hand with something out back."

"I'll return, my love. Don't go anywhere."

Elsa remained on the porch by herself. She thought over everything—everything that had happened to get her to that exact moment. It seemed strange, but it all seemed to fit together. However difficult, she sensed that this journey was meant to be. She had been constructing a puzzle, where all of the pieces had a place, a purpose, and a reason. Now she could see herself as a part of the picture, she was a piece of that puzzle to make her family portrait complete.

Then Elsa thought about the power and influence of the past, which had clung to claim its rightful domain within her present life. It was not merely the past, but also those spirited and eccentric ancestors from a bygone era who haunted a future of which they could never truly be part. Had the spirits longed for her company, as their offspring and therefore proof of their prior existence, or had they simply longed for life?

Elsa heard Gustavo calling to her. She walked around the house to find the family standing in the backyard. "Come, Elsa. Hernán is going to show us the silkworms."

The family walked through the darkness to reach the shed. Hernán entered first and pulled a cord hanging from the ceiling to turn on the single light bulb. They all stepped into the room. The family walked around the beds of silkworms. Miguel said, "Look at this one, and at how it twirls itself around."

Josephine and Lina huddled together, watching a worm busy at work constructing its cocoon. Lina pointed and said, "Look how fine its thread is, and how it shimmers."

Then they all gathered around a bed of moths that were busy mating. They flapped their wings eagerly. The soft light in the room shone off their translucent wings, and then it seemed as if the moths were lifting out of the bed, reaching toward the ceiling, toward the light of the single bulb.

And later, as the family continued to laugh and weep, dream and sleep, through the days of their lives, the silkworms in the shed continued silently to weave their magical cocoons. In the dark shadows, women gathered in a circle around the cauldron of boiling water, gently tugging at the cocoons with tongs, unleashing their abundant golden threads that stretched for miles and miles. The shimmery delicate threads unraveled, only to wrap and twine themselves together to become strong and resilient. Then they would braid once again into a magnificent, glowing cocoon that would encase the family in light and a deeply ancient, mysterious love.

About the Author

Claire Ibarra is a writer, poet, and photographer. She received her MFA in creative writing from Florida International University. Her work can be found in many fine literary journals and anthologies. Claire's poetry chapbook *Vortex of Our Affections* was published by Finishing Line Press in 2017. She lives and teaches in Colorado.